A NANTUCKET AFFAIR

NANTUCKET BEACH PLUM COVE SERIES

PAMELA M KELLEY

PIPING PLOVER PRESS

"What do you think? I'm not sure if I like this or the other recipe better?" Lisa took another bite of the artichoke and spinach quiche. It was a new recipe, and it was delicious.

"I like it. Maybe a little more than your other, although that's really good, too. Sorry, I'm no help." Her best friend, Sue, laughed and helped herself to another small slice. It was early, just a quarter past eight, on Friday, and she and Sue were heading off-island to do some shopping. Sue was taking a rare day off, and they were planning to have lunch in Hyannis and maybe see a movie before hitting Trader Joe's and then taking the late afternoon Fast Ferry back to Nantucket.

"This is good, but I think I actually like your other recipe a little better. Something is different about this one. A missing spice, maybe?" Angela said. She always shared breakfast with Lisa before heading upstairs to clean the guest rooms. Angela hadn't been on the island long, less than six months, but she'd quickly become like a member of the family. Angela's life had changed so much since she left San Francisco and moved to Nantucket when her grandmother, whom she had never known, left her a cottage on Nantucket. Angela's original plan had been to make a few repairs, sell the house and move back to San Francisco.

But then she met the Hodges family, and through them, Philippe Gaston. Now, the two were practically engaged and Angela decided to stay on Nantucket—which Lisa was very glad about. She enjoyed Angela's company, and it was a godsend having her do the cleaning. Lisa still did it on Angela's days off, but it was a huge help to have someone else do it most of the time. Her knees and back protested when she did it more often.

And fortunately, her home, now also known as the Beach Plum Cove Inn, had a steady business going. With the help of her son, Chase, she'd turned the five upstairs bedrooms into guest rooms and served breakfast each morning in the dining room for those who wanted it. She always had a selection of juices, coffee, breads, pastries, cereal, fresh fruit and usually one hot item, like a quiche.

Usually, her fiancé, Rhett, was the first one to breakfast, but he was away for a few days visiting his daughter and his other restaurants. They'd met when Lisa first started the bed-and-breakfast, and Rhett was her first guest. He liked to joke that he came and never left. But it was true. He came to open a restaurant in Beach Plum Cove, their area of Nantucket. And he and Lisa were both surprised to find themselves drawn to each other as neither was really looking. Rhett proposed at Thanksgiving, moved out of his guest room and into the main house with Lisa.

"So, it sounds like you two have a fun day planned," Angela said.

Lisa smiled. "We do. It's been ages since we've done this. Sue's business is booming, so we've had to reschedule a few times."

"It has been crazy, but in a good way. Brandi is working out so well."

"Brandi is the pretty blonde girl you pointed out a while back?" Lisa hadn't actually met her, but thought she remembered Sue mentioning when they were out to dinner a few months ago that a woman sitting at the bar with an older man worked for her.

Sue nodded. "Yes, she's a gorgeous girl. Long blonde hair, a figure I'd kill for and big blue eyes. Though she's in her early thirties and we all looked much hotter then." She laughed and patted her stomach which, like Lisa's, had grown a bit soft over the years.

"She's done a great job, though. She just landed a huge client. You know the Lawson family? Cory

Lawson runs Lawson Financial Group, a hugely successful hedge fund. They are insanely rich, and Brandi closed him and now we are handling all their insurance needs. And the policy for his business is one of the largest we've ever written."

"That's incredible." Lisa was happy for her friend. Sue and her husband Curt had started their insurance firm when they were first married. Curt handled sales while Sue did all the back end operations of running the firm. They had a bustling office right on Main Street with about a half-dozen people working for them, but Sue mostly worked from home. In addition to the insurance firm, she also ran a related online business, a new venture that she was having a lot of fun with, and it was easier for her to focus at home. When Lisa had once asked if she missed working in the office, Sue had said that she got so much more done at home without people constantly interrupting her.

"I know them. I just started cleaning for the Lawsons a few weeks ago. Mandy is really nice. I haven't met her husband Cory yet, though. She said he's a workaholic and is never home."

"Kate and Kristen graduated with them. I think they were high school sweethearts and married young, right after college. They've done well for themselves. Chase mentioned that he is going to be doing a kitchen remodeling project for them soon. He said their house is stunning." Lisa's son, Chase, was a successful contractor.

"They bought that house a few years ago. I remember when it went on the market and one of the girls in the office brought in a real estate brochure. It looked like something out of the Great Gatsby, with French doors that opened out to a sunroom that was practically hanging over the ocean. Just gorgeous."

"They are so young to be so rich. I wonder if they're happy?" Angela said.

Sue chuckled. "How could they not be with that much money?"

Angela smiled. "Right. I just can't imagine it myself. Not to that level, anyway."

"You have quite a business going now, too. You might need to hire people soon to help you handle all your new clients." Lisa was proud of Angela, and how well she'd done. She recommended her to everyone she knew as Angela was the best cleaner she'd ever used, and it was clear that she enjoyed the work. She'd worked as a cleaner while putting herself through college and was finishing up her last few classes online. Her original plan had been to get a job in marketing at a tech company in Silicon Valley. But now, she was using what she'd learned to market her own cleaning business.

Angela grinned. "I already have hired two people."

"That's fantastic. Is one of them Harriet?" Lisa had told Harriet, the woman who had cleaned for her before she went to Jamaica for the winter, to call Angela. Her original plan had been to hire her back if she could, but now she had Angela who could work year-round, and she liked her company each morning.

"No, but she did call, and I told her to just get in touch when she's back for the season and I can probably keep her busy."

"That's wonderful."

When they finished breakfast, Angela headed upstairs to start cleaning, and Lisa and Sue set off for the ferry.

———

LISA LOVED TAKING THE HYLINE FAST FERRY. THE Grey Lady grew bigger every few years as demand grew. The Steamship Authority was the other option, and they only used that if they were going to take a vehicle off island—which they were not doing, because the nickname for the Steamship Authority was the 'slow boat'. It took just over two hours to make the trip, and they much preferred the Hyline, which was half the time. It would be easy enough once they got to Hyannis to get an Uber or Lyft to do their shopping.

They had a lovely day, hitting the mall and the Barnes and Noble bookstore. Nantucket had several lovely independent bookstores, but Lisa loved to go to Barnes and Noble when she was off-island as the selection was huge. As much as she loved living on Nantucket, there were limitations, and many more of the bigger stores and businesses were on the mainland.

The movie theater was ten times the size of the one on Nantucket and after a delicious lunch at Tiki Port, a Chinese restaurant right across from the mall, Lisa and Sue saw a new romantic comedy they'd heard good things about.

They stopped at Trader Joe's on the way back to the ferry and stocked up on all their favorite snacks. Lisa particularly liked a cheddar cheese that had a hint of parmesan flavor, and she picked up a few bottles of Josh Cabernet when she saw that it was a good three dollars cheaper per bottle than on Nantucket. Everything was more expensive on Nantucket.

When they were settled on the ferry and waiting for it to depart, Lisa took a sip of the chardonnay that Sue had bought for her. The boat had a full bar, and it was nice to sip a glass of wine as they made their way back to the island. Sue frowned as her phone dinged to announce a text message.

"Is everything okay?" Lisa asked.

"Oh, it's fine. Curt just let me know that a few of them are heading out to dinner. He didn't think I'd mind since I won't be back until after six."

"Do you mind? You could probably join them? What will you do for dinner?"

"No, I don't mind. We went out for lunch so I don't need to go out to dinner, too. I have plenty of food at home. I'm just annoyed with Curt in general. That's part of the reason I wanted to take today off. I just needed a break. I'm sort of hating him today."

Lisa laughed. She knew her friend didn't really hate her husband. She and Curt had been together forever. They'd met in college and married a year after graduating. Curt's family was from Nantucket, and Sue had fallen in love with it the first time she visited the island. They were both finance majors and at first, Curt worked as an accountant in the family practice and Sue got an entry-level job at an insurance agency. She'd loved the work and ten years later, when their two children, Travis and Stephanie, were in elementary school, the owners of the insurance agency asked if she might be interested in taking over the business as they were eager to retire.

She and Curt discussed it and decided to invest in the new business and work there together, and it had worked out well. Curt was outgoing and energetic, and it turned out that sales and account management suited him well. Sue was the opposite, quieter and more organized. So, it worked, but like any marriage, occasionally they got on each other's nerves.

"What did he do?" Lisa asked.

"Well, you know how stubborn he can be sometimes? He insisted that he was going to pay the club membership. That he wouldn't forget. I said I'd be happy to do it, but he insisted. And then, of course, he forgot, so we have to pay a late penalty. And also, he hates to go out to dinner. I always have to beg him if I want to go and then he usually orders a burger and complains that everything is too expensive."

Lisa laughed. He did do that.

"I don't think he appreciates food the way we do. He likes everything."

"He does. And now he's going out to dinner. It's just frustrating because whenever I suggest it, he rarely wants to go. And to make matters worse, he announced a few weeks ago that he needs to get rid of some extra weight, and just like that, he's already down twenty pounds."

"Ouch. That really isn't fair. How did he do it?" Lisa could sympathize. It seemed like it was always easier for men to lose weight.

"He just stopped eating anything white. Skips breakfast. Doesn't eat lunch and is now terrified of carbs, apparently. But it's working for him."

"Ugh. That doesn't sound like fun. I'd miss carbs."

Sue laughed. "I know. I would, too. It's fine. I don't really hate him, of course."

"I know you don't. And you got some delicious stuff at Trader Joe's."

"I did. I'm looking forward to putting on my sweats, maybe having another glass of wine and diving into the jalapeno and cilantro hummus we just bought."

"That sounds good to me, too."

CHAPTER 2

It was nearly nine by the time Curt finally got home. Sue was in her pajamas by then, and curled up on the sofa watching the movie Jerry Maguire for the third time while polishing off a pint of Ben and Gerry's Cherry Garcia. She raised her eyebrows at Curt when he walked in the room.

"Well, hello there. Dinner was fun?"

Curt flopped on the love seat adjacent to the sofa that she was lying on.

"It was a good time. I didn't realize it was so late. You don't care, right? I figured you'd be tired after shopping all day."

Sue sighed. "No, it's fine. Lisa and I had a big lunch today. We had fun. Who all went to dinner?"

Curt grinned. "The usual suspects. Bill and Tom, Mary and Brandi." Bill and Tom were the other agents in the office. They were in their forties, both married with children. Mary was the receptionist, and Sue was surprised that she went out with them. She usually rushed home to get dinner on the table for her husband. Brandi didn't surprise her. She was always up to go out. Sue wondered how she liked Nantucket, and if there was enough here to keep her around more than a year or two. She supposed it depended on if she met someone that she could be serious with. She imagined that Brandi probably wanted to marry and have kids and her window of opportunity for that was narrowing, as she was already in her mid-thirties.

"I'm surprised Mary went out."

"I was, too. Her husband is out of town."

"Ah, that explains it. Where did you go?"

"Brandi wanted tacos. So we went to Millie's and practically closed the upstairs bar. It was a good time."

Sue loved Millie's. They had the best Mexican food on the island and it was California style, so more authentic and a bit lighter, with really fresh ingredients.

"I'm glad you had fun." A thought occurred to her. "What did you eat? Mexican isn't very diet friendly."

Curt laughed. "You're right. It was hard not sharing the nachos that they ordered for the table. I just had a piece of fish and some veggies. It was fine."

Sue shook her head. "I don't know how you do it. I couldn't have resisted."

Curt patted his stomach proudly. "Down twenty-two pounds as of this morning. Eight more to go. I'm fitting in pants now that I haven't worn in years."

"Congrats." The weight loss was definitely noticeable. Curt looked leaner and toned, too. She frowned as she took a good look at his slightly brown face.

"Have you been tanning?" The gym that they belonged to had a tanning bed, but neither one of them had used it before. As far as she knew.

Curt looked a little embarrassed. "Yeah, I checked it out the past few times I was in the gym. Figured why not try it out? I read somewhere that you look thinner with a tan."

Sue shook her head. "I didn't realize you'd been hitting the gym that often."

"Yeah, I started back up again about a month ago, after I lost my first ten pounds. I suddenly had more energy and wanted to get back in the routine of going."

Sue wondered when he was fitting it in, and realized he probably went at lunch, instead of eating. Since she was rarely in the office, she'd had no idea.

"That's good. I should probably get back there one of these days myself." They had a family membership and Sue cringed whenever she'd get the occasional email from the gym, saying how much they missed her and inviting her to come in soon for a workout or a smoothie. She felt guilty for not going, but still didn't get in there. And it was irritating to think that now Curt was regularly working out again.

"I don't think that tanning beds are all that good for you."

Curt grinned. "Everything in moderation, right?"

"Right. Well, I'm off to bed. Are you coming?"

He hesitated. "No, I'm going to stay up a bit. I'm not really tired yet. I'll see you in the morning."

CHAPTER 3

"All right, I'm ready to hit the road. I'm meeting the guys at the McCarthy project this morning and I'll be in Siasconset at the Jones's new construction this afternoon. Anything else you have lined up for me?" Chase Hodges sipped from an aluminum thermos of coffee as he waited for Beth, his office manager and girlfriend, to respond.

"Mrs. Granberry is expecting you at eleven for an estimate on her kitchen remodel and don't forget, we're meeting Lauren at two at 68 Bayberry Road." Beth handed Chase a slip of paper with both addresses.

"Oh, that's right. That's today. That one sounds almost too good to be true. At that price, offers will probably go over the asking price, don't you think?" He was trying not to get his hopes up as the property Beth had found seemed perfect for them for their new hobby, flipping houses.

It was Beth that had first suggested the idea. She was always on the internet and knew about all properties the instant they hit the market. As his office manager, it helped for him to know what was being sold and for what price as his main business was new construction and remodeling. Flipping houses was the perfect side hustle.

Flipping on Nantucket was especially lucrative, as there was a bigger demand than supply and prices were sky high for even smaller properties. The trick, though, was getting a property for the right price and getting it before someone else did. There were other contractors on the island looking to do the same thing. So, the houses they bid on often went for above the asking price, and they always needed a lot of work. Usually the condition of the homes scared off most buyers, and that's when Chase and Beth found the best deals.

"I'll check in with you later. I won't make it back here for lunch. Too busy of a day."

Beth smiled. "That's okay. I'll see you at two."

Chase gave her a kiss goodbye and headed out. He was looking forward to seeing the house with Beth later that day. She had a good eye for bargains, and so far, they'd done two flips and not to his surprise, they made a great team. Beth found the houses, he did the remodel work, and she helped him with all the design work, suggesting how the kitchen should look, what tiles in the bathroom, paint colors everywhere and then she staged it so that it looked amazing and had an upscale, Nantucket flair that buyers couldn't resist.

They made quite a team, and he'd never been so happy since he realized that Beth was more than the best office manager he'd ever had. And he almost lost her, too. He'd thought he was head over heels for Lauren, the realtor that they were meeting later. Lauren was blonde and beautiful, driven and very used to having her own way. He was never really happy when he was dating her, though, as Lauren was a handful and he never really knew where he stood with her. Which, of course, drove him crazy.

But it wasn't until Beth gave notice and moved off-island that he'd realized what an idiot he'd been. And the person that he spent the most time with, his office manager and best friend, Beth, was the person that mattered most to him. Fortunately, he came to his senses, went after Beth, and now things were as they should be. She was the one he wanted to spend the rest of his life with—and he planned to make it official soon.

BETH WAS A LITTLE WORRIED THAT THEY MIGHT NOT GET this house. The location wasn't on the ocean, which was a very good thing. Those houses were way out of their price range. Even the disasters that needed to be totally gutted went for insane prices simply because of the land.

This one was about a mile from the beach, which meant the cost would be much more reasonable. Most of the developers seemed to go for the big wins, whereas she and Chase went for the less obvious ones. The ones that needed a lot of work, but that didn't scare them.

She loved managing Chase's business, and she'd been doing it for years now, talking to all of his clients and potential clients, being aware of everything that was going on and helping to keep things on track. But the flipping was a new thrill. It was exhilarating, and she loved everything about it…finding the hidden gem that made for a good flip, and winning the house. They didn't always win. Sometimes they were vastly overbid. But that was part of it, and they were fairly conservative with their bids as there was almost always hidden expenses that came up. And even though Chase could do all the work, unexpected surprises usually meant more materials that needed to be purchased or additional people that needed to be paid for their time.

So, she was cautiously optimistic about this one. If they both liked it, they would make an offer on the spot with Lauren, and hopefully their speed would give them an edge. Unless the seller wanted to wait for additional offers, which they often did.

<hr />

AT A FEW MINUTES BEFORE TWO, BETH PULLED UP TO

the house on Bayberry. Lauren was already there. Beth recognized her white BMW. The house had looked better online. It was a clear, sunny day and the bright light showed the fading paint and the failing roof. It looked like the house had been empty for a long time, as there were weeds along the edge of the side porch, and the trim was cracked in spots. But these were all fixable things.

"Hi, Beth. Good to see you!" Lauren walked over with a big smile. Beth liked Lauren. She was very good at what she did and had given them an early heads up on their last property. She was so polished and put together, with her sleek, blonde bob that fell in a perfect, razor-sharp line to her collar bone. She was wearing an expensive-looking outfit, with tailored gray pants and a pretty blue top. And as always, she was wearing strappy high heels. Beth always felt a bit frumpy around her as she wondered, not for the first time, how she managed to get around in those shoes. Beth was dressed for comfort in faded jeans, a warm, oversized sweater and comfy Merrills black suede clogs, her staple shoes in the colder weather.

Chase pulled up in his truck a minute later and came bounding over.

"Hey, sorry I'm late."

"You're not," Beth assured him.

"We just got here, too," Lauren said. "Are you ready to head in?"

"Looks a little rough," Chase said softly to Beth as they followed Lauren inside.

"I thought the same," Beth agreed. "But, aside from the roof, it looks like mostly cosmetic stuff, on the outside anyway."

Chase grinned. "Right. Will be interesting to see what awaits inside."

AT FIRST GLANCE, THE INTERIOR OF THE HOUSE DIDN'T seem too bad. It obviously hadn't been lived in for some time.

"Do you know when someone last lived here?" Beth asked.

"It's been a few years. The owners bought it as a summer home, but they live in New York and haven't made it here for the past two seasons. They were thinking about renting it out, but they know it needs some work and just didn't want to deal. My brother knows the owner somewhat. They went to school together. They are pretty motivated for a quick sale now."

That was somewhat reassuring to hear that Lauren, or her brother, personally knew the owners. A friend of Beth's had found herself in a nightmare situation in Texas when she and her boyfriend had bought a house that was also from motivated sellers and they quickly learned that there were some major issues that hadn't been disclosed, like tree vines growing into the septic that was a disaster to fix—and Texas was a buyer beware state, so even though they took them to court, they really had no recourse and lost quite a bit of money,

Lauren led them through the house. It had three bedrooms, all good sized, and the master bedroom had its own bathroom. There was another bath and a half, though they were both really dated and downright ugly.

"We'll have to totally gut and redo all the bathrooms," Beth said, and Chase nodded as he made note of it on his iPad. He filled out an estimate form as they went through the house, so they'd have it to refer to later as a ballpark idea of what they'd be looking at for costs.

The kitchen was also going to need a total overhaul. Everyone these days wanted white kitchens, and this one was dark wood with avocado green appliances. Chase made a face when he saw them and looked at Lauren.

"When was this built?"

She glanced at her data sheet. "1972."

He laughed. "That's what I figured. At least there's no shag carpet." The floors were all hard wood but they were in poor shape, full of scratches in different areas. Beth guessed that whoever had lived here had a dog. And it looked like the sealing on the floors hadn't ever been redone. The floors were swollen in spots and uneven.

"We'll have to replace the floors. It looks like they had some water damage at one point."

The living room was a big room, with a fireplace, but it was closed off from the kitchen. It was the older style home where all the rooms were closed off. Buyers these days all wanted open concept.

Chase assessed where the walls were. "It doesn't look like this one is load bearing, which is a good thing. We can knock this down and open up the living room to the kitchen and add a big island here, with a few stools."

Beth nodded. "Good, I was hoping you'd say we could do that. A good island makes the kitchen."

"I sold a gorgeous one last month," Lauren said. "The island was oversized and looked like it was marble, but it was one of those quartz countertops that are more durable. It made the kitchen look stunning."

Beth looked at Chase. "We could do something like that here."

"We could." Chase walked into the next room, which was meant to be a den or an office and stopped in his tracks. "It smells like something died in here."

Beth followed him into the room, and her eyes immediately started to water. "It does. What do you think it is?"

Chase walked all around the room and stopped in front of a small closet. He leaned in and took a good look. "I think I found the problem. There's a small door here that goes to a crawl space. A squirrel or something might have gotten stuck."

"That's disgusting." Lauren wrinkled her nose and quickly left the room. "I can call the owners and tell them to get someone out here to investigate and exterminate or whatever they need to do. But, that might take a little time and more people might get wind of the property. Right now, you're the only ones that have seen it."

"Give us a minute," Chase said and pulled Beth aside.

"What do you think?"

"Aside from the smelly closet, it's actually better than I thought it would be. It looks like your biggest expense will be the roof?"

Chase nodded. "That's what I was thinking, too. We can use our credit line to make a cash offer today and close in a few weeks. And I could line up an exterminator to clear up the closet issue so it's done before we start work."

"I think if we could get this house, it could be an awesome flip." Beth hoped that a close-to-asking-price offer could do it.

"Okay, we're ready to make an offer. We'll do five thousand under asking, as we'll have to get that dead smell situation cleared up before we do anything else. But we can pay cash and close in two weeks. I can give you a check for the deposit now."

Lauren looked pleased. "I think that's an excellent

offer and I'm assuming you'd want to get someone in to exterminate before we close?"

Chase nodded. "Ideally, yes. The longer that sits, the worse the smell will be." He wrote out a check and handed it to her.

"Great. Thanks. Let's get this offer written up and hopefully we'll have a fast answer. I know he's looking to get this done ASAP."

LAUREN CALLED THEM LATER THAT EVENING, AS BETH and Chase were sharing a pizza at home and watching a movie on Netflix. Lauren's voice was so loud and excited that Beth could hear everything she was saying to Chase.

"Congratulations! The house is yours. And they're thrilled it's a cash deal. We can close in two-and-a-half weeks."

"That's great news, thanks." Chase hung up and lifted his glass of water. "Cheers! We got it."

Beth tapped her glass of water against his and couldn't stop smiling. "I didn't think we'd hear so quickly. I'm really excited for this one."

Chase chuckled. "You're always excited for them."

"Oh, I know. But I have a really good feeling about this one. I can't wait to see how the kitchen remodel turns out."

"It's a good time of year, too. Summer is right

around the corner and if we do it right, this could sell quickly."

Beth grinned. "And then it will be time to find another house to flip!" She quoted the line that ended every episode of one their favorite HGTV house flipping shows.

CHAPTER 4

"What do you think about an early September wedding on the beach?" Lisa topped off both her and Rhett's glasses with a little more cabernet and set the bottle on the kitchen island. They had been snacking on cheese and crackers. The kitchen smelled heavenly as a big pot of meatballs and homemade sauce simmered on the stove. Neither one of them was in a hurry to eat, though. It was nice to just catch up. Rhett had been gone for almost a week, the longest amount of time that they'd been apart since she'd met him. And while she didn't mind an occasional break, she'd missed him more than she expected to. The house felt empty without him, and so much nicer now that he was home.

"Sure, that sounds fine to me. You know I'm okay with whatever you want to do." Rhett reached for a slice of cheddar and popped it in his mouth.

"I know, thanks. I don't want anything big, as we've both already done that. But I thought maybe a small gathering, just close friends and family. It's so nice here in September, after Labor Day, when the weather is still gorgeous and the crowds are gone."

"Works for me."

"I thought I could get Kate and Abby to help me organize it all. They're both really good with all the details." Kate worked at home as a writer, doing occasional freelance articles for the magazine she used to work for and also writing mysteries. She also handled the marketing for the inn and did an amazing job of it. Thanks to Kate's expertise with Facebook ads and other internet marketing, the inn stayed steady with bookings.

"That sounds like a good plan," Rhett agreed.

"Well, I think Abby might be ready for a project. Jeff doesn't want her to go back to work. She wants to stay home with the baby, too, but it can be a little isolating. She does such a good job coordinating the food pantry events."

"Mm." Rhett reached for more cheese and Lisa laughed. He was obviously hungrier than she'd realized.

"Are you ready for meatballs and pasta?"

He smiled. "I could eat."

She fixed bowls of pasta and meatballs and set them on the island, along with a hunk of parmesan cheese and a grater.

"Oh, I have bread, too, if you want it."

She went to get up, but Rhett shook his head. "I'm good. I got on the scale this morning and let's just say I should skip the bread for a while."

He looked absolutely fine to her. But she also knew how it felt when an extra five pounds crept on.

"I think you look fine, but I understand. Sue was just telling me that Curt has dropped twenty pounds recently by cutting out bread, all carbs apparently. She said he's not eating much at all and the weight is falling off fast."

Rhett grated a pile of cheese onto his pasta. "Good for him. I wouldn't go that far, though. I actually saw him earlier today getting coffee downtown. He looks like he's been on vacation. Did they go away somewhere?"

Lisa laughed. "No. Sue said he's been using the tanning bed at the gym. Thinks it makes him look thinner."

Rhett raised his eyebrows. "Maybe I should try that?"

Lisa was pretty sure he was kidding. "Don't you dare!"

He chuckled. "I thought you knew me better than that."

"I can't imagine you in a tanning bed."

"Neither can I. So, what else did I miss while I was gone? Anything new with the kids?"

"Yes, Chase and Beth found another house to flip. It's a fixer-upper on Bayberry Road."

Rhett thought for a minute. "Is it the one right on the corner, blue with a porch?"

"I think so. Do you know it?"

"I've driven by it a few times and it stuck out like a sore thumb. Looks like it's neglected and needs a lot of work."

Lisa worried for a minute that maybe they'd taken too much of a risk, but then dismissed the thought.

"I'm sure it's fine. Chase knows construction and Beth, too. They wouldn't have bought it if they weren't sure it would be a good investment."

"I'm sure you're right. I just had some friends that used to do a lot of that kind of thing, and now and then they got in over their heads and ended up under water, taking a loss. But, like you said, they know what they're doing."

CHAPTER 5

The light coming through her oversized windows was fantastic, and on most days that would have meant an excellent painting session, the kind where Kristen would lose herself in her work and hours would disappear. But not today. She was struggling to get the vision in her mind onto the canvas in front of her. She knew that part of it was because she had a hard stop at four. She couldn't let herself lose track of time today. The girls were all coming over for an appetizer night and drinks, which was always a good time. But, she was also worried about Tyler.

He lived in the cottage next door and they'd been dating for about six months now. Everything had been going so well. He was an artist, like her, a best-selling mystery author, so they understood each other's obsession with their work and need for plenty of alone time.

Tyler was the complete opposite of his brother Andrew, who Kristen had actually dated a few times before she met Tyler.

Andrew owned an art gallery downtown, and she'd enjoyed his company. He was also passionate about art and extremely social and outgoing. A typical extrovert. But he was her rebound person. They'd dated immediately after she'd broken things off with Sean, who she once thought she wanted to marry. But Sean was on a different timeline. He was separated when they met and never got around to filing for divorce—until she broke up with him. He begged her to reconsider, and she felt like she had to give him a chance.

So she did, but it didn't last long. Everyone else saw it before she did, but Sean was completely wrong for her. And when he finally did propose, she had the sense to say no and to end things once and for all. And Sean got over it quickly enough as a few months later, he was engaged to someone else—someone who was actually much better suited for him. Jessica was equally interested in money and power and being seen as successful, just like Sean. Kristen had no interest in any of that. She was just happy that she was able to support herself with her painting.

And Tyler was the same way. He was actually a best-selling author and had an avid fan club on Facebook—women of all ages, many in their fifties and sixties, who thought he was the cutest thing and their favorite author. Kristen thought they had excellent taste. She'd liked Andrew, and they remained good friends when she went back to Sean. By the time they broke up, Andrew was dating someone else pretty seriously and Kristen had a small pang of regret as Andrew made her laugh and was fun to be around. But when she met his brother, who had just bought the almost identical cottage next to hers, she felt instantly drawn to him. They'd been pretty much inseparable ever since.

She was worried about him recently, though. He and Andrew unexpectedly lost their mother over the holidays, and Tyler had taken it hard. They'd both been very close to her. Tyler needed long stretches of time for his writing, but they usually saw each other almost every night. And he still seemed to be very down. He was quiet anyway, and she knew that sometimes he was just in his head with his book, trying to work out a plot problem and dreaming about the rest of the story. But something seemed off lately. She was surprised that he was still so withdrawn and distant. And he pushed away her attempts to help. She'd suggested a week ago, not for the first time, that he might want to talk to someone, a therapist or grief counselor. He'd immediately dismissed the idea.

"I don't need a grief counselor. I'm fine. Just sad sometimes, but I'll deal with it."

She wasn't going to see him tonight because the girls were coming over, but she was planning to make a lasagna and figured she'd make two and bring a tray over to him. The girls were all bringing the appetizers and a salad. She glanced at the clock, and it was a quarter to four. She was going to quit for the day at four, but it had been such an unproductive session that she decided to call it a day, and went to the kitchen to start on the lasagna.

Her mother had stopped by the day before for a visit and dropped off a big container of sauce and meatballs, which Kristen put to good use with the lasagna. She mixed together the ricotta cheese, parmesan, spices and an egg and layered it between sheets of curly-edged pasta, sliced mozzarella and sauce. She'd serve the meatballs on the side. After she slid the two trays of lasagna in the oven, she jumped in the shower to clean up.

By the time she was dressed and finished blow drying her long hair, which took a while, the kitchen smelled incredible. A short while later, she could tell by the smell that it was just about time for the lasagna to be done. She checked, and they were bubbling and golden brown on top, perfectly done. She carefully slid them out of the oven and set them on the stovetop to cool. It was almost five-thirty, and the girls were coming around six. She should have time to run some lasagna over to Tyler. She was looking forward to seeing him for a few minutes, too. She loved spending time with him. She didn't want to just drop by, though. She hated when people did that to her as once she was interrupted, it was difficult to get back into the same artistic zone again.

At a quarter to six, when the lasagna was slightly cooler, she called Tyler. He didn't pick up right away. She thought it was going into voice mail, but then he answered.

"Hey, there."

"How's your day going? I just made some lasagna for the girls and I have an extra tray. I could bring it over for your dinner." She knew Tyler loved all pasta and thought he'd be thrilled, but he surprised her.

"Thanks, but I think I'll pass. I figured out a plot issue and I don't think I'm going to break for a while. I'll probably fall into bed after that, I'm beat." He did sound exhausted.

"Oh, okay. Totally understand. I'll talk to you tomorrow."

Kristen hung up and felt bad that she'd clearly interrupted him while he was working. But, he didn't usually work this late in the day. Tyler tended to be an early writer, getting most of his words down first thing after he woke. But sometimes, he did go back for a second session toward the end of the book. He said that's when the words always came faster. But, she'd thought that he was in the early stage of a new book. Oh, well. She could bring it over to him tomorrow and they could have dinner together. Lasagna always tasted better the next day when the flavors sat overnight.

She put a sheet of foil over the extra tray of lasagna and moved it into the refrigerator. The girls should be arriving any moment, so she opened two bottles of wine —a Josh cabernet and a Bread and Butter chardonnay. She loved both, but would be having red with the pasta, and she knew Angela and Abby preferred white.

They'd all kind of adopted Angela since she moved to the island. She was the youngest of the group, at twenty-nine, but as an orphan who had grown up in the foster home system, she had an old soul, and Kristen had felt like she'd known her forever. She was so glad that Angela took over the cleaning for her mother. She said that she actually enjoyed cleaning, which Kristen couldn't imagine, but she'd said that she found it calming and satisfying to bring order to clutter and chaos.

She also cleaned once a week for Tyler, which was working out great. He had a tendency to let things pile up and then complained that he was blocked. Kristen suspected that having a clean, calm environment helped to free up the mind to be more creative. But she had to laugh because they were both the same in that when they were deep into their work, they managed to be quite messy. Kristen always cleaned up immediately after a session, but Tyler tended to put it off, and some-times needed Angela to come twice weekly when he was going fast and furious with his writing.

Abby and Beth arrived at the same time. They were best friends. Beth had stopped by her house after work, and they drove over together. Everyone was thrilled that Chase had finally come to his senses and realized that Beth was the one for him. It had been obvious to everyone else, and Beth had been pining for him for years—and he had no clue. Men could be so oblivious at times. Angela arrived a few minutes later and then Kate was last, came rushing in and apologizing for being late.

"I'm so sorry. I lost track of time and burned the first batch of cookies. Well, I actually left them for Jack, as he said he doesn't mind when they're a little black on the bottom. But the second batch came out much better." She set another bottle of Josh and the container of peanut butter chocolate chip cookies on the kitchen counter.

"That means the writing was going well?" Kristen hugged her sister hello.

"Yes! Finally. The past few days have been slow, but it's picking up speed again. What did everyone else bring?" Kate was the foodie in the family and loved to cook as much as their mother did.

"I made my mother's clam dip recipe," Beth said. She took the lid off a bowl of creamy white dip studded with bits of clam and dusted with chopped parsley.

"You made the clam dip?" Abby asked. "That is so good. I didn't think I was going to like it the first time I tried it, but wow."

Kristen was curious to try it, too. Like Abby, if she

had to be truthful it didn't really sound all that good. But maybe she would be surprised.

"I made guacamole and homemade California-style salsa. I hope you all like cilantro." Angela laughed as she set her bowls on the counter.

"I made the garlicky white bean hummus again, with lemon and parsley. You all seemed to like it last time we got together." Abby had a platter with chopped fresh veggies and pita chips in a circle around a bowl of vibrant green hummus.

"Oh, good! I loved that. And it's sort of healthy, right?" Kristen joked as she dipped a pita bread into the hummus. It was smooth and rich and lemony and garlicky at the same time. "What does everyone want to drink?" She took their orders and poured wine for everyone while they brought all the food over to her big kitchen table, and they spent the next few hours chatting and snacking on all the appetizers.

Beth told them all about the newest house that she and Chase had found to flip.

"It should be a good project. It needs more work than the others we've done, but I don't think it's anything Chase can't handle, stuff like a new roof and opening up the living room."

"So it opens into the kitchen? I love open concepts," Angela said.

"Yes, exactly. Everyone wants that these days. It's going to be a fun one to decorate as we are redoing it all—new bathrooms, a totally new kitchen, the works."

"That sounds expensive," Kate commented as she dipped a chip into the clam dip, trying it for the first time. Kristen hadn't ventured in yet either and waited to see what her twin sister thought. They often liked the same things. Kate's surprised smile indicated a thumbs up and she confirmed it. "This is so much better than I expected. Sorry, Beth. I was a little apprehensive of clam dip, but this stuff is addicting."

Beth laughed. "That's the typical reaction. The key is to chop the clams up small, use plenty of the juice, which really just gives a salty flavor, and lots of cream cheese, sour cream and Worcestershire sauce."

Kristen followed her sister's lead and had to agree. "This is really good."

Beth went back to Kate's comment about the project sounding expensive.

"It is our most expensive renovation to date, but we think we got the house for a good price and should still see a good profit at the end."

"I can't wait to see it when it's all done and decorated. Will you do an open house, like the others?" Angela asked.

For the past two flips, that had been exactly what Beth and Chase had done. They'd worked with Lauren as their realtor, and as much as Kristen disliked her as a girlfriend for Chase, she recognized that she was an excellent and savvy realtor. Lauren had suggested the strategy of holding an open house the first weekend the property was on the market.

They held a private realtor open house the week before and said that no showings would be held until after the open house.

Once they saw the house and the gorgeous renovation job, the realtors had all scrambled to bring their best clients to the open house, and Chase and Beth received multiple same-day offers. Kristen hoped the same thing would happen with this house. The thought of spending so much money made her nervous, though. Kristen was the most conservative one in the family, as she'd had to learn how to make her money stretch in between sales of her paintings.

Beth nodded. "Yes, I'll let you know once we schedule the open house. We're aiming for just before or after July Fourth." The island was always packed that weekend, so assuming all went well, they should have plenty of traffic for the open house.

"Angela, how is everything going with your business?" Kate asked. Once Angela had decided to stay on Nantucket, she put all of her energy into finishing up her last few college courses online and building her cleaning business.

"It's going better than expected, actually." She grinned. "I never would have imagined that studying marketing would help me to do cleaning full-time. I do love it, though. I've hired a few more cleaners, both full and part-timers, and I'm planning to target the summer market, the people that are here in their huge, gorgeous homes for the season or even just a week or two. I can help them get the houses all cleaned and ready for them when they arrive."

Kristen was impressed. "That's a great idea. And I bet there's a big need for it."

"It seems like there might be. I talked to a friend of Rhett's that runs a placement network of sorts. He fields calls from hotels and restaurants mostly, looking for people. But he said he also gets calls from visitors looking for private chefs or house cleaners and he can't always service them. So he may send some referrals my way. And it gave me the idea to reach out and target those people directly, too."

Kate looked intrigued. "That's brilliant. Are you using Facebook ads to do some of your marketing?"

"I'm starting to. So far, I've mostly just visited local realtors and given them my business cards. I may want to pick your brain a bit as I know you've done a great job for the inn."

"I'm happy to show you what I'm doing. Let's get together soon for coffee and I can walk you through it."

Angela looked grateful. "Thank you, I'd love that."

"How are things going with Tyler?" Abby changed the subject. Kristen suspected that the business talk bored her.

"It's going pretty well. He still seems to be dealing with his mother's death, mostly by keeping to himself and focusing on his writing. Which isn't a bad thing, I suppose. It gives him something to direct his energy toward."

Abby frowned. "That doesn't sound overly healthy. I've seen Andrew out and about, and he seems to be doing well. He's always so upbeat and friendly."

"Andrew is the complete opposite of his brother. He's all light and sunny, while Tyler is more dark and moody. Tyler's a much better fit for me, though."

"Oh, I know he is. I didn't mean to imply anything. I like Tyler, too. It just seems like maybe he should talk to someone. Has he been to a grief counselor or anything like that?"

Kristen shook her head. "No. I suggested it, but he wants no part of going. I think it's a guy thing, maybe. They think it's a sign of weakness. I'll suggest it again, though, when it feels like the right time to bring it up. He shut me down fast when I mentioned it just a few days ago."

"Maybe he just needs some time to get used to the idea." Something flashed across Angela's face that Kristen couldn't decipher. The expression was gone seconds later, though, and she wondered if she might have imagined it. It was probably nothing—but everyone also knew Tyler's history. He was a recovering alcoholic and so far, as long as Kristen had known him, he'd successfully stayed on the wagon. But she'd worried about the possibility of a relapse and what she would do if it happened. Could she handle that? And how could she support him? Hopefully it was a non-issue, though, as it had been nearly six months and she imagined that if his mother's death was going to trigger a relapse, that it would have happened already.

Later on, after they'd all had their fill of lasagna and the delicious cookies that Kate had made, everyone eventually called it a night. Angela was the last to leave, after jotting down her guacamole and salsa recipe for Kristen. Kristen loved cilantro and wanted to make it the next time she had Tyler over for dinner.

"Thank you. Has Tyler been having you come twice a week lately?" she asked as Angela handed her the slip of paper with the handwritten recipe.

Angela smiled. "Yes. He's needed it, too. He apologizes for the mess each time I come, but says it's because the story is consuming him." The same expression Kristen had noticed earlier flashed across her face again, but was instantly gone as Angela looked down for a moment. Kristen felt a sense of unease, and a worry that she was missing something with Tyler.

"Have you noticed anything different lately when you've cleaned?" Kristen wasn't really sure what she was asking, but something seemed off with Tyler unless this was just him going through the stages of grief, his own way.

Angela hesitated and looked like she was debating whether to say anything. Finally, she just smiled. "He's messier than usual. I do think maybe he's still having a hard time with something. I mean with his mother's death, obviously. I would definitely try to get him to talk to someone. That helped a good friend of mine in San

Francisco, when he was…" She paused for a moment, choosing her words carefully. "When he was going through a hard time."

"Okay, thanks. I was planning to keep on him. I don't want to be too much of a nag, but I think it's important."

Angela gave her a hug. "I think you're right to be concerned. I hope that he gets the help that he needs."

CHAPTER 6

Sue slept in Sunday morning and when she rolled out of bed a little before nine, she was surprised to see that Curt was already up and dressed. She was half-awake as she padded downstairs to the kitchen, made her first cup of coffee and raised an eyebrow as Curt gathered his briefcase and coat.

"Where are you off to? We have lunch with Mom today."

"I'm heading to the office to meet Brandi and a few others on the committee for A Nantucket Affair. It's the only day that worked for everyone and we have a lot to do. I thought I mentioned this to you last week."

He might have. Sue didn't pay close attention to all the different charity things that Curt was involved with. She was happy to write the checks for them, as she knew they were all for good causes and good PR for the agency. But Curt loved getting involved and A

Nantucket Affair was his baby. He'd chaired the committee for the past few years, and Sue had to admit that he and his team always did a great job. The event was held in the middle of July, a catered affair on the beach, with music, usually a celebrity guest or two and a silent auction.

"I'm sure you did, and I just forgot."

Curt smiled and his dimples popped as laugh lines danced around his eyes and mouth. "Give Mom a kiss from me."

"I'll tell her you said hello. Have fun."

"You, too," he said as he walked out the front door.

Sue sighed. Lunch with her mother was usually anything but fun.

HER MOTHER WAS WAITING ON THE FRONT PORCH OF Dover Falls, the high-end retirement community. She was dressed in her Sunday best, one of her many Talbots outfits—gray tweed skirt, matching jacket and a cream-colored silk blouse, the pearls that she always wore and a gold Nantucket basket brooch pinned to her lapel. Her one casual concession was her favorite pink sneakers instead of the patent leather pumps she usually wore. Sue knew that meant that her feet were bothering her again. She was prone to painful bunions. Sue felt her mother's pale blue eyes assessing her as she approached the porch steps. She gave her a quick hug and sat in the empty chair next to her.

It was a lovely retirement home, and her mother was on the assisted living side. She didn't need a lot of help, but stairs gave her difficulty. Two of her friends lived there and had enticed her to join them.

"You look like you've put on a few pounds."

Sue sighed. "Hello to you, too, Mom, and I'm the same weight I've been for the last few years. Curt sends his love. He couldn't make it today."

"Hm. Well, you look a little soft, dear. Do you still go to that fancy gym?"

"I haven't been in ages," Sue admitted. "I've been meaning to get back there. Curt has been going. He's lost over twenty pounds." Although it was frustrating that it seemed so easy for him, she was proud that he'd done it.

"Really? Twenty pounds? That's interesting."

Sue laughed. "And he's been using the tanning bed, too. He's become even more vain with how he looks." Curt had always been a sharp dresser, and was a handsome and charismatic man. Even though he'd been annoying her lately, she still recognized that most people found him quite charming.

Her mother looked like she was about to say something, then turned her head and looked out over the tops of the trees, to the sliver of ocean visible on the horizon. Slowly, she lifted herself from her chair.

"Let's go into the dining room."

Sue followed her inside. Her mother had a lovely villa that had everything she needed, including a small kitchen, but like most of the others, she took all her meals in the main house dining room. And Sue didn't blame her. Why cook if she didn't have to, and the food was unusually good. The chef had worked at some top restaurants on the island and Dover Falls had recruited him to run the kitchen. Sue had thought it interesting that a chef at that level would be interested. He'd even once run the ultra-exclusive new country club kitchen for a few years. But he once told her mother and her friends that this was pretty much his dream job now. He had free rein to make whatever he wanted and his hours were much better—instead of being at a popular restaurant until midnight or later, he mostly worked a regular day shift and as soon as the evening meal was served, his day was done.

There was always some kind of roast for Sunday dinner. Today it was roast beef with mashed potatoes, gravy, glazed carrots and popovers that were light as air and served with honey butter. Sue could have easily eaten a second popover, but it wasn't worth the look her mother was sure to send her way.

They chatted about anything and everything as they ate. Her mother caught her up on all the goings on at Dover Falls, and apparently there was a lot of drama. One of her friends had broken up with her boyfriend and was already dating a new resident that had just arrived two weeks ago. It was evidently quite the scandal.

Dessert was a chocolate mousse that her mother

daintily picked at, while Sue inhaled hers.   As her mother sipped her coffee, she turned her attention back to Sue and Curt.

"I don't want to suggest that anything is improper, but in my experience, when a man suddenly loses weight and takes extra care with his appearance...such as tanning, which is so ridiculous that I hardly have words, it's a red flag. Have you considered the possibility that there might be someone else he is looking to impress?"

Sue set her coffee cup down so hard that a few drops splashed onto the snowy white linen table cloth.

"No, that never entered my mind. It's Curt." They'd been married for over thirty years and had two kids together. "I know him, Mom."

"Hm. Right. Well, the wife is often the last to know, or the last to admit what is right in front of her."

Sue shook her head. The very idea her mother was suggesting was ridiculous. Yes, she'd been annoyed with Curt from time to time, but their marriage was solid compared to a lot of people she knew. Surely, she'd sense if something was going on.

"I think you're just being paranoid. My life is boring. Nothing like the soap opera that you are living in here." Sue chuckled.

"You're probably right, dear. I always did have a vivid imagination. It keeps things interesting. Where is Curt today? You didn't mention why he couldn't make it."

"He's at the office with Brandi and a few others on the committee for A Nantucket Affair."

"Oh, that's right. He's in charge of that event. I always liked that one. And Brandi, she's the new girl you hired a while back?"

"She is. She's doing a great job and just landed us a new, big client. She's Curt's co-chair on the committee."

Her mother added a bit of sugar to her coffee, gave it a stir, then took a slow sip. "Well, isn't that nice of her? How old is she?"

"Mid-thirties, thirty-five or thirty-six. I don't remember which."

Her mother nodded. "And she's a pretty girl? Is she married?"

"Very pretty. Long blonde hair and a figure I'd kill for, not an ounce of fat on her." Sue smiled. "And she's not married. I suspect she'll find someone pretty quickly. At least I hope she will, otherwise I don't imagine she'll stick around very long."

Her mother looked thoughtful. "Yes, for your sake. I hope she does find the right person soon. It sounds like she might be hard to replace."

Sue was always surprised by her mother. For someone who had never worked, she had always had a good head for business, and Sue had often run things by her over the years.

"Yes, that's very true. It will probably be hard to find another Brandi."

CHAPTER 7

Lisa met her other best friend, Paige, for a late lunch, early dinner on Sunday at the Club Car. Rhett was going to be at his restaurant all day and into the evening, so when Paige suggested getting together, she didn't hesitate. Normally, they would have included Sue, too, but Lisa knew she was having lunch with her mother. She always did the first Sunday of every month. More often, too, but always the first Sunday, without fail.

Paige spent her winters in Florida, but cut it a little short this year because she was anxious to get back to Nantucket to see Peter. He owned Bradford's Liquors, and the two of them had been friends for years until they were both surprised when it took a romantic turn over the holidays. Lisa was pretty sure the two of them were madly in love, though Paige was being quite calm about it all. Lisa suspected she was afraid to jinx it, as things were going so well and Paige had been single for a long time. The two of them were thick as thieves, though, and though Paige had been back from Florida for almost two months, Lisa'd only seen her twice.

"So, things are still going well with Peter, I take it?" Lisa asked once they were settled and had each ordered a glass of wine.

Paige smiled and her eyes lit up as she talked about Peter. "I can't believe it's been over six months now since we started dating. It feels longer and yet like it just started at the same time, if that makes any sense."

Lisa nodded. It meant her friend was head over heels for Peter. She was glad to see it. Paige was one of her dearest friends, and Peter was a nice guy. He'd lost his wife of many years to cancer a few years back and had been slow to consider dating anyone again until he and Paige got to chatting one day when she stopped into the store and asked for a wine recommendation.

"He went to see you in Florida?"

"Yes. He took a whole week off in February and came to see me. Said it was the first time he'd taken a real vacation in years."

"I'm happy for you. I like Peter."

Paige laughed. "So do I."

They put their lunch orders in when the server returned with their wines. Lisa got the lobster salad roll and Paige lobster salad, no roll.

"Are you dieting?" Lisa asked. Paige had never had a weight problem as long as she'd known her. She was tall, naturally blonde and slim. She also did yoga all the time and recently started teaching classes a few times a week. Lisa kept meaning to go and try a beginner class. She was nervous because of her back and knees, but Paige insisted that it could help strengthen them and loosen her core muscles, which would help ease her aches and pains.

Paige laughed at the thought. "No, I just never eat the roll. I don't want it to get in the way of the lobster."

That was true. Paige always had ignored it. Lisa loved the combination of sweet lobster on a buttery hot dog roll, toasted to a golden brown.

"So, I think I might be ready to try one of your classes. Let me know which one is for absolute beginners and I will be there."

"Excellent. Tomorrow at ten. Should I call you at nine to remind you?" Paige knew her well.

"No, I'll be there."

They caught up on all the local gossip over lunch and had just ordered coffees and a crème brûlée to share when both of them turned at the sound of loud laughter at the bar. It was almost five, and the place was getting busier. There was a group of six or so at the end of the bar. One man surrounded by five or six women who seemed to be hanging on his every word. A pretty blonde woman had her arm around the back of the man's chair and was whispering something in his ear. He then repeated it to the others, and they all broke into hysterical laughter again. The blonde woman moved her head back and Lisa recognized her as Brandi, and the man as Sue's husband, Curt.

"That's Curt, isn't it?" Paige asked with narrowed eyes.

"Yes, and Brandi from his office. I'm not sure who the others are."

"I thought he'd be with Sue, visiting her mother."

"I assumed the same. Maybe it's a work thing," Lisa wondered.

"Maybe. That's interesting body language, though. Look how she keeps leaning in and touching his arm. Maybe that's just how she is."

"Could be. He's the same way. Curt's always been a big flirt, but it's harmless. He just likes women, loves the attention."

"I'm glad Peter's not like that," Paige said.

Lisa was thinking the same thing. "Rhett's not, either. I don't think Sue minds, though. She trusts Curt. Though he has been annoying her more than usual lately, it seems."

"Oh?"

"You know how she is. He gets on her nerves, sometimes. She usually ignores it, then he'll do something inconsiderate, and she'll call and tell me she hates him. But she's just venting and doesn't really mean it."

"Marriage isn't easy. All that compromising. I have to admit, I like not living together with Peter. We each have our own space, though we see each other almost every day and spend most weekends together either at my place or his. But I like having a few nights totally to myself. And I think he does, too."

"I can see that." Paige had lived alone for so long that Lisa knew she was somewhat set in her ways.

"I'm the opposite. I like having Rhett living with me. I missed him when he was gone for a week. The house felt empty."

"Well, as much as I enjoy Peter's company, I also didn't mind being by myself in Florida." Paige grinned. "I just didn't need to stay there as long as usual."

After they paid their bill and were about to leave, Lisa glanced over at the bar. Curt was still holding court and smiling at Brandi, who had her hand on his arm and was chatting away. To anyone who didn't know better, they might assume they were a couple.

IT WAS STILL BOTHERING LISA A LITTLE A FEW DAYS later. She didn't think there was really anything to it, but if she was Sue, she'd want to know if her husband was getting a little too chummy with someone.

So, when Sue called the next day to see if Lisa wanted to meet up for coffee downtown, Lisa mentioned it. They were sitting in a cute cafe on Main Street. Both ordered orange scones and non-fat lattes. Because Sue worked from home, she liked to get out once or twice a week in the late afternoon for coffee. Lisa liked to get out of the house, too, so it worked out perfectly. They usually walked around downtown for a bit after, strolling down to the docks and watching the ferries come and go.

"So, I saw Paige yesterday. We met up for a late lunch at the Club Car. I knew you were seeing your mom. How is she?"

"She's good. Same as ever. Told me I could lose a few pounds."

"Ugh. We all could. You look fine. Don't pay any attention to her." Sue's mother had always been critical, and it didn't help that she'd always been trim. She'd never worked and Sue's father had been well off, so her mother was part of a crowd of other ladies who lunched, and never left the house without looking perfectly polished from head to toe.

"I'm used to it. Sure, I could lose a few pounds. But, I like to enjoy life, too. I don't want to give up anything, like Curt with his sudden fear of carbs. No, thanks."

"Speaking of Curt, we saw him on Sunday, at the Club Car. He was at the bar with a group of women. I was surprised. I assumed he'd be with you and your mom."

But Sue didn't seem fazed in the least. "He's the chair again of the Nantucket Affair committee. I know they were meeting in the office that day. They must have gone for drinks after they finished up. Brandi was probably with him?"

"She was, yes. And four or five other women."

Sue smiled. "I think Curt is the only guy on the committee. He must have been in his glory surrounded by all those women."

"He didn't seem to mind it."

"That explains why he went to bed so early. He said he wasn't hungry for dinner and fell fast asleep on the sofa watching TV, a little after seven. Must have been the drinks."

Lisa was glad that Sue didn't seem concerned by Curt's behavior. It had looked a little off to her, but what did she know?

CHAPTER 8

C hase always stopped by the office with Beth before heading off to whichever project he was needed on. But he never stayed for long.

"Okay, I'm off. I should be able to break for lunch around noon. I can pick up subs for us, if that sounds good? Tuna with lettuce, pickles and hots for you?"

Beth nodded. "And a bag of chips. I can't eat tuna without chips."

"Got it. See you in a few hours." Chase left and Beth turned her attention to the computer screen. She'd been on the Houzz site, and Pinterest before that, getting decorating ideas for the house. In between answering the phone and other work she needed to get done for Chase, she kept looking for the perfect colors and tiles for the bathroom. If it was her own house, to keep, she'd go for more vivid colors and patterns. For a flip, they needed the look to be elegant and fashionable but not too much, and the colors to be neutral, mostly soft blue grays and creams. The house had to be attractive but the buyers needed to see it as a blank slate, so they could make it their own. It was a fine line, and a challenge that Beth loved.

She'd always enjoyed the work she did for Chase. She was his right hand, talked to all of his clients, and acted as a project manager of sorts, directing where Chase needed to be, and putting in most of their orders with the suppliers. Her strength was planning and organizing, while Chase's gift was working with his hands. He had a reputation for high quality work, at reasonable prices. He mostly worked by referrals and it kept him very busy.

It had been Beth's idea to try the first flip. She'd always been careful with money, not much of a spender, and she'd accumulated a good amount of savings. Her original intention had been to use it for a down payment on a house someday. But now that she and Chase were living together, she wasn't in a hurry to use the money for that. She hoped, at some point, they might build a house of their own and start a family. But until then, it was tempting to put that money to work.

They were both addicted to the HGTV shows on flipping, and Chase had once commented that it would be a really cool thing to do and that he had the perfect background for it—but then he never mentioned it again. Beth filed the comment away, though, and kept an eye out for a potential investment property.

That first opportunity came their way one day when Beth was chatting with Bob, one of their clients, who mentioned that his mother had recently died after a long illness and a stay in a nursing home.

"I had a realtor come and take a look and they gave me a long list of things I needed to do to get it into shape to sell or I'd never get the right price. I just don't have the energy to oversee that right now. I might just tell her to sell it as is, I suppose. I'm not much looking forward to that, either."

"Can you tell me more about the house? Where is it? What kind of work did she say it needed?"

"The location isn't too bad. It's a small lot, about a half mile walk to the beach. It needs some roof work, mostly replacing shingles, not a whole roof. The rest is cosmetic but there's a lot—according to the realtor, all the wallpaper has to come down, and I see her point there. The carpets are all worn and need replacing. There's some mold in the bathroom, the venting seems off. There's more, but that's the gist of it."

"Could we take a look at it? We could give you an estimate and you could decide what to do?"

"Sure. Why not?" They agreed to have Chase stop by the next day to do a walk-through and put an estimate together. On their way home from work that day, Beth told him about the house and they drove by to take a look at the exterior.

"This could be an opportunity for us, to do our first flip—if you think it makes sense, once you work up an estimate. Keeping in mind, of course, that the cost you quote him will be less for us."

"He won't want to have us do the work and sell it himself?"

"We'll give him that option, of course. But he's exhausted and just wants to be done with it and put it behind him. We could make him an offer, as another option—if it feels right to you. I have a bit of money saved to invest, too."

"You do?" Chase sounded surprised, and she didn't blame him. They'd never discussed any specifics about their financial status.

"Yes, I'm a good saver." She told him how much she had in her account and his eyes bugged out.

"That's almost as much as I have. I'm impressed. And you'd really be willing to invest some of it? You could lose it all."

Beth smiled. "You're the best investment I can think of. We won't do this unless we're sure of it and that we leave plenty of margin for error. For unexpected expenses."

When they met Bob the next day to tour the house, Beth's excitement grew as they went from room to room. The house was small and needed a lot of work, but it was mostly all cosmetic, besides the mold in the bathroom from poor ventilation. Chase gave Bob a quote and his face paled.

"I'll be honest with you. I don't really have the time,

energy or the money to do this. I guess I'll call the realtor and just tell her to sell it as is."

"What price did she suggest?" Chase asked.

"Not as much as I'd hoped. But it's better than nothing." He mentioned a number that was quite a bit lower than Beth expected. She could tell by Chase's eyes that he felt the same.

"Bob, could you give us just a minute?" Beth pulled Chase outside and they quickly agreed on a price to offer Bob—a bit more than what the realtor suggested as they figured if it went to market, it would likely go above asking.

"Bob, if you're interested, we'd like to make you an offer for the house." Chase mentioned the number he had in mind, and for the first time, Beth saw a look of hope on Bob's face.

"Are you serious? If you are, I gladly accept your offer." He looked around the house. "Will you keep it? Or fix it up and sell?"

"Fix it up and sell. It's something Beth and I have been looking to get into."

"Well, it sounds like it's a win for all of us, then."

———

AND IT HAD BEEN. THEY LEARNED SO MUCH DOING THAT flip. Beth had enjoyed every minute of it. She was proud of the design work she'd done, and Chase's remodeling had made the cottage absolutely adorable.

They'd modernized it and added an island in the kitchen—all new appliances, white subway tile, which gave it a clean, bright look—and they added French doors where the sliders had opened to a big screened-in porch. They'd also redone the bathrooms completely, bringing in an expert to remove the mold, add vents, and sleek, glass shower doors which gave it a spa feel.

When they gave the listing to Lauren, she'd been impressed, as she'd been the realtor Bob met with initially, so she'd seen the 'before'. Once the open house was held and they accepted one of the multiple bids, they realized a bigger profit than they'd expected. And from then on, she and Chase were addicted.

Lauren actually found them their next flip. It was a similar situation, a smaller home that needed lots of cosmetic work to be attractive to buyers. Most people wanted something turnkey that didn't need a lot of work. She showed them the home a few days before a scheduled open house, said the buyer was motivated and if the offer was good enough, they'd accept and cancel the open house.

"I'd really rather not do an open house, if I don't have to," Lauren admitted.

And that one had been a no-brainer, too. Chase agreed and less than two months later, Lauren sold the house again for a much higher price. Beth and Chase were feeling a little cocky after the second flip went so well. It almost seemed too easy.

She hoped that this third house would go as

smoothly. She didn't see why it wouldn't. Chase was already aware of all the repairs that needed to be made. As long as they didn't find any surprises along the way, they should be looking at another healthy profit in a few months.

CHASE RETURNED TO THE OFFICE A LITTLE AFTER NOON, with the subs and chips for their lunch. They sat at a small round table in his office and spent the half hour enjoying their lunch, chatting about the progression of the various projects Chase had going. Just as they were finishing up, his cell phone rang.

"This is Chase. Oh, hey, Barry. So what did you find in there?"

Beth watched as Chase's expression shifted from amused to concerned as he ended the call and told Barry he'd be right there.

"Is that Barry Holmes, the exterminator?" Beth knew they had him going to check out the smell in the closet and to remove whatever had died there.

"Yeah. He said it's a family of squirrels, four of them, that crawled in somehow and got stuck there. While he was removing them, though, he found something he wants me to take a look at. Something to do with the pipes. Might be nothing, or might be kind of expensive as I'd have to hire someone to do that work."

"Well, let's hope it's something minor." Beth felt a

twinge of worry, which she quickly brushed aside. Chase would be able to handle it, whatever it was.

Chase took his last bite, crumpled up the paper wrapping and tossed it in the trash. He handed her his almost empty bag of chips.

"Here, finish these off. I'm going to head out. I'll fill you in later."

CHAPTER 9

"So, I have an idea I want to try. An experiment with some different targeting on FB. Do you mind if I change the ads up a little?" Kate asked. She and Lisa were sitting at Lisa's kitchen island. Kate had come by for lunch and to chat with Lisa about her Facebook ads for the inn. They were sitting side by side, with their laptops in front of them.

"Sure, honey. Whatever you want to do is fine by me. You know I appreciate your help. It's all Greek to me." Kate understood the ins and outs of internet marketing, especially Facebook advertising, far better than Lisa ever would.

While Kate played with the ads, Lisa scrolled through the recent reviews that guests had left on AirBnb, the site that generated many of her bookings. They were always mostly four- or five-star reviews, except for the occasional grump. Now and then, they had a guest who was difficult and impossible to please. There wasn't enough hot water or the water was too hot, the sheets were too soft or not soft enough. It seemed like some people were just looking for things to complain about. But fortunately, that was the rare exception and most of the guests had been lovely.

"Hmmm. This is an odd one. This couple was so nice and yet they left me a one-star review."

Kate looked up. "What does it say?"

"It's the strangest review we've had yet." Lisa read it out loud.

"Location was lovely, but the service was disappointing. The host, Lisa Hodges, seemed as though we were bothering her at breakfast when we asked for decaf coffee. We won't be back. Next time, we'll stay at Red Rose Bed and Breakfast. We usually stay there and tried something new this time and that was a mistake. Don't make the same mistake we did. Go to Red Rose."

"Hm. Wasn't the owner of Red Rose one of the people that opposed you at that first selectman's meeting?"

"Yes. She was." Lisa sighed. "Maybe the Laceys are friends of hers. Or maybe they really were disappointed."

"That review almost reads like an ad for Red Rose."

Lisa bit her lower lip, something she did when she was deep in thought or worried.

"Do you think that will hurt business?"

Kate hesitated for a moment before saying, "Well, it's not helping. Negative reviews like that can deter people, which seems like the intention. You should reply to it."

"Really? What would I say?"

"The best way to handle a negative review is to kill them with kindness, and to try to make it right. Even if they don't reply, others will see that you care about customer satisfaction. Ask them to message you directly with their concerns and say that you will do what you can to make it right. If they do, offer them a free night if they give you another chance."

Lisa frowned. "The last thing I feel like doing is giving them free anything."

"Remember, Mom, this is a business decision. I know this hurt your feelings. It would mine, too. But don't take it personally."

"It's hard not to. But, you're right. I'll let you take a look before I hit submit."

Lisa thought about what to write and then kept it simple. She read it aloud to Kate when she finished.

Thank you for staying with us and for sharing your concerns. I'm so sorry that you were disappointed with the service. We try our best to make every guest feel welcome, but we're not perfect. I hope that you will give us another chance. Please message me to discuss how we can make your next visit a better experience.

"That's perfect," Kate said.

Lisa hit submit and sighed. The bad review had spoiled her good mood. She was feeling very down and like a failure. She got up and cut herself a slice of the cinnamon walnut coffee cake she'd served that morning to the guests. It was decadently rich, made with butter and sour cream, and Lisa usually avoided it or had the tiniest of slivers. The guests always loved it. Instead of a sliver, she cut herself a thick slice and asked Kate if she wanted any.

"No, thanks. That will go right to my hips and I don't need any help there."

Lisa smiled as she settled back in her seat and took a big bite of the cake. It was perfect comfort food and she'd always been a stress eater. Kate was exaggerating a bit, too. She'd never had a weight problem, though she wasn't as slim as her sister, Kristen, who wasn't as food obsessed as the rest of them. Kristen often forgot to eat while she was painting.

"Mom, seriously don't give too much weight to that review. It's just one review out of a sea of positive ones. Everyone loves staying here."

"I suppose you're right."

"I am. And I understand, believe me. It's even worse with writing. There are always people that just don't like what I write, no matter how much everyone else loves it. It took me a long time to realize that they just aren't my audience. I cried when I got my first bad review. I made the mistake of looking at reviews before writing, and I wasn't able to write a word that day, I was so upset."

"Oh, honey. I'm sorry. You're a wonderful writer. Ignore those mean reviews."

Kate grinned. "Exactly. That's excellent advice, so you do the same."

Lisa laughed and felt her bad mood fading.

An hour later, as Kate was getting ready to head home, Lisa's mailbox dinged with a new email. It was from Ron Lacey, who must have seen or been notified about Lisa's reply to their review. She steeled herself for more negativity when she opened the message, but Ron surprised her.

"Lisa, I have to apologize. I'm not sure what came over my wife to leave that review. We had a great stay and everything was just fine, better than fine. I'm embarrassed to admit this, but Debbie is friends with the owner of that other bed-and-breakfast. She must have been trying to help her. I will make sure the review is amended, or removed. And I thank you again for a great stay. Ron Lacey."

"Oh, how interesting," Kate said.

"Do you suppose Lillian put her up to it?" Lisa asked. She couldn't imagine deliberately trying to harm someone's business that way.

"It wouldn't surprise me. Unfortunately, from what I've heard online it's a thing. Competitors try to sabotage the competition by leaving bad reviews or trying to direct traffic their way by mentioning their name in a review for a competing product."

Lisa was shocked. "And that's allowed?"

"It's against the terms of service, but it's not always obvious or easy to enforce. People have a right to their opinion, even if it's a negative one."

"Hm. Well, I guess I'm lucky then that he offered to fix it."

"You really are. That seldom happens."

"I knew Lillian wasn't happy about my new business. She obviously thinks it's a threat to hers."

"It looks that way. But hopefully this is a one off, and won't happen again."

That thought hadn't crossed Lisa's mind. "Ugh. Hopefully not."

"I'm sure it won't. Don't worry about it. I'll keep you posted how the new ads go." Kate gave her mother a hug and headed back home.

Once she was gone, Lisa put on her sneakers and walked down to the beach. It was cool but sunny, and she could use a long walk down to the lighthouse and back to work off some coffee cake. Walking along the beach always lifted her spirits, too. She loved the salty smell of the air coming off the water, and the soothing crash of the waves as they hit the sand. Every time she walked along the beach, she felt better and couldn't imagine living anywhere else.

CHAPTER 10

Barry was waiting outside having a smoke when Chase pulled up to the house. He took a final puff, then put the cigarette out with the heel of his scuffed boot.

"How bad is it?" Chase asked when he reached the front steps.

"I'm no plumber, but I don't think it looks good." Barry led the way to the closet. He'd disposed of the dead squirrels and already plugged an air freshener into the wall, so the scent of lavender mingled with death as Chase entered the room.

"Take a look." Barry stepped back and handed Chase his flashlight.

Chase kneeled down and trained the light on the hole in the wall and the exposed steel pipes that were not in good shape. They were rusted at all the joints.

"Did you check the water?" He asked Barry.

"Color is good, nice and clear, but the pressure is low."

Chase frowned. When he'd toured the house with Beth and Lauren, he'd checked the kitchen faucet and the water pressure seemed fine. He hadn't bothered to check the bathrooms. But he did that now, and all the faucets were all the same, very low pressure.

"You thinking what I'm thinking?" Barry asked.

Chase sighed. "Yeah, I'm probably looking at a full re-pipe. No one uses steel much anymore, but all these older houses have it and they always have to be replaced at some point. Looks like it has to be now on this one."

"What do you think that will run you? You're doing this as a flip, right?"

Chase nodded. "I'm guessing between eight and ten thousand. Hopefully not more than that. I usually use Rick Cushman for plumbing. I'll see if he can get out here tomorrow. And yeah, this is a flip, so it's not ideal to have to sink that kind of money into it, but what are you gonna do?"

Barry smiled. "Yep. Well, at least it won't stink of dead squirrels."

"There is that." Chase had his checkbook with him so he wrote out a check for Barry, and as they left, he put a call into Rick.

BETH HAD EXPECTED CHASE TO CALL HER AFTER HE met with Barry, but she didn't hear from him until he returned to the office at the end of the day. She could tell that he was in a bad mood the minute he walked through the door. Chase was so seldom in a bad mood that it took her by surprise.

"Is everything okay? I thought you would have called after your meeting," she automatically asked before he said anything.

Chase sighed and ran a hand through his hair. It was thick and wavy and normally one of his best features, but today it just looked rumpled and frazzled, much like Chase himself.

"No. Sorry I didn't call. I had to go right to the Johnson site and put out a fire there. One of the vendors is holding up the project and we're running a little behind. You know I hate that."

Beth nodded and waited for him to continue. Chase prided himself on finishing his projects on time or earlier.

"So, yeah, I met with Barry. There's a plumbing issue. Probably needs a re-pipe. I called Rick and he's going to take a look tomorrow. Re-pipes are expensive and we didn't plan for that in our budget."

Beth mentally did the calculations in her head. She knew the going rate for a re-pipe and conservatively estimated high. Even if it came in at ten thousand it would be a hit to their budget, but they could still potentially be okay—as long as there were no other unexpected surprises.

"We can work with that. If we need to, we can cut costs in other areas, maybe go with less expensive tile or counter tops."

Chase frowned. "We still need it to look high end though, or we won't get the price we need."

Beth took a deep breath before speaking. "I know that. We'll figure it out." She tried to stay calm and not let her irritation show. Hopefully, Chase would relax about it. She knew he was just worried and she was, too. Neither one of them could afford to lose money on the flip. But she didn't think that was going to happen, as long as they were smart about how they allocated their budget.

"Yeah, it's still early days. You're right. No need to panic yet. Sorry, I'm being grumpy. It's been a long day, and I'm hungry. How do you feel about pizza for dinner?"

She relaxed and smiled. "Pizza sounds good to me."

BETH CALLED IN THE PIZZA ORDER BEFORE THEY LEFT the office so that it was ready for them to pick up on their way home. She and Chase liked their pizza the same way—plain cheese, extra sauce. They also got a Greek salad to share.

Once they were home and happily eating pizza, Chase seemed to relax a bit. Beth couldn't remember ever seeing him so stressed before. She worried that the flip house and its unexpected expenses were making normal stress from his job seem worse than it was.

"So, tell me what's going on with the Johnson project?" Last she knew they were running a little behind, but she thought Chase was going to catch up this week.

"Well, I was hoping to get back on track this week, but we've fallen further behind. Two of Shaw's guys missed work this week, both sick and they didn't have anyone else to send, so until they get their part of the job done, it's holding up moving forward on other stuff. It's just frustrating. Ben apologized up and down, even said he'll come help himself when he's done with his current project."

"Well, that's good then. That should help them get it done faster."

"It should." Chase reached for another slice of pizza. "You know how I am about finishing on time."

Beth smiled. "Yes, I know." Chase had built his reputation on doing quality work and meeting project deadlines. It was somewhat unusual in an industry when so many workers were self-employed and were often either stretched thin by taking on too many projects or took too much time off fishing when the weather was good. It was so bad that when someone like Chase came along that was reliable and good, word spread quickly. It also helped that Chase was an island native and most people either knew him or his family, so there was added trust there.

"I'd like to go with you tomorrow when you meet Rick at the flip house." Beth had been thinking about it all afternoon. "I think it could help me to better understand everything that goes into doing a renovation like this. And I want to get some more pictures of all the rooms and measure the counters and floors."

Chase hesitated for a moment, caught off guard by the request, but then nodded. "Sure, that's actually a good idea."

"I have them now and then," she teased and was pleased when he cracked a grin. His earlier bad mood was totally gone.

He put his slice of pizza down and leaned in to give her a quick kiss.

"I don't know what I would do without you."

"You'd fall apart, totally."

He laughed. "Seriously, I might. I don't want to ever find out."

"Well, you don't have to worry about that. I'm not going anywhere." She stood and cleared her paper plate and glanced at his. She wasn't sure if he was going in for another slice or not, but he slid his empty plate toward her and she threw them both in the trash. Then she went to the freezer and pulled out a carton of vanilla fudge ripple.

"Did you save room for ice cream?"

The easy smile that she loved so much slid across his face.

"What do you think?"

She scooped ice cream into two bowls, and they took them into the living room and settled on the sofa to watch a little television. Beth sat sideways and rested her feet on Chase's lap. His ice cream was gone in two seconds, and as she'd hoped, he started rubbing her feet while she slowly savored the rest of her ice cream. Chase gave the best foot massages.

A few minutes later, she was feeling totally relaxed and glad that they'd both managed to help the other to relax. She'd always thought they'd make a good team and they had for years, but now that they were together romantically, it was even better. They complemented each other and she'd been pleased to point out to Chase recently that she'd looked at the numbers and since they officially became a couple, the business was more profitable too—up 10% overall. It could be a coincidence, of course, natural growth of a solid business. But she liked to think that it was partly because they were now a team, in all ways, and that carried over to the business.

That was just an added plus, though. It had been somewhat of a risk for the two of them to date and work together. But Beth had known in her heart that it would work, that they would work. She'd known long before Chase had. He'd finally came to his senses and she had to give him credit—he'd tried to make up for lost time. They got along great and never fought about anything. She'd admitted that to Abby once. She and Chase's younger sister were best friends, and Abby had been surprised.

"You never fight at all? No disagreements ever?"

"Well, of course we disagree occasionally, but it's always little stuff. Nothing important and there's never any anger there."

"Hm. You do know that's not entirely normal, right? People fight. You must still be in your honeymoon phase."

Beth didn't think so. "I don't know about that. We just get along. Maybe it helps that we were friends for so long first."

"Maybe. I am happy for you both. And maybe a tiny bit jealous. Jeff and I get along great, but we sometimes have rip-roaring fights. He can be a jerk sometimes." She smiled and added, "And he'd probably say the same thing about me. But we both love each other dearly. It's all good."

Beth was glad that she and Chase never fought. She knew a lot of couples did and that it was normal and healthy, but she liked things the way they were. So far, their relationship was going as well as she'd imagined—better, even. A few friends had expressed concern when she'd told them that she was going back to working for Chase and that they were going to start dating. They worried that either their relationship or her job would suffer if they spent that much time together.

But that was one thing Beth had been confident about. She knew how well they worked together and she loved her job. She felt like a true partner to Chase and found real satisfaction in understanding his business and working with their clients. And there was no shortage of conversation between the two of them. Now and then, they laughed and said that they really should stop talking so much about work when they were home, but the reality was they both loved it, so it was something they were always eager to talk about. And now, with a few successful house flips behind them, there was even more to discuss.

CHAPTER 11

Kristen was surprised and pleased when Tyler called the day after she'd had the girls over and suggested dinner out at his favorite restaurant.

"I take it the writing is going well?"

"I'm a quarter of the way in now and the story is starting to hum along. It's been a good couple of days and now I'm craving prime rib."

Kristen laughed. She knew Tyler was like her in that when they were deep into their work, they sometimes forgot to eat.

"That sounds good to me. I'm just about done for the day, too, and heading into the shower."

"Great. I'll swing by around six."

Tyler drove and when they reached the airport restaurant, it was busy but not as crowded as most places downtown would be. Crosswinds was a casual, pub-like environment and a popular spot for the locals. The food was reasonably priced and consistently good. When they were settled at their table, Kristen ordered a glass of cabernet and Tyler surprised her by ordering water.

"No O'Doul's tonight?" He always ordered O'Doul's non-alcoholic beer when they went out.

He smiled and she noticed he was tapping his fingers on the table. One of his nervous habits. She hadn't seen him do it in a long time.

"Just not in the mood for beer. Do you know what you're going to get?"

"I'm not sure." She had barely looked at the menu and turned her attention to it so she'd be ready when Lori, the waitress that usually waited on them, returned with their drinks.

She set their drinks down in front of them a few minutes later. "So, do you need another minute or two to decide?"

"I'm ready," Tyler said.

"I'll do the chicken pot pie." Kristen folded the menu shut. She'd had the pot pie before, and it was always good.

"Prime rib for me, medium."

Lori put their orders in and a few minutes later, set down a basket of rolls and two salads.

Kristen reached for a hot roll. "So, the writing is going well now?" She was glad for him. Tyler had struggled with the beginning of his newest book and she knew it was stressing him out. He was quite a bit behind schedule.

"It is, finally. It's starting to come together. I wasn't sure if it ever would. It's never been this hard before," he admitted.

Kristen knew it was his mother's death that had thrown him off in so many ways. He was still hurting from the loss, and it had affected his creativity, too.

"Is it starting to get a little easier?" She reached out, took hold of one of his hands and gave it a gentle squeeze.

He nodded, understanding what she meant.

"A little. There's not as much darkness now. But it's still hard. You know how close we were?"

Kristen nodded. Both Tyler and his brother, Andrew, had adored their mother and talked to her several times a week.

"That's the hardest thing. If I'm having a good day or a bad day, I reach for the phone to call her and then realize she's not there."

"I'm sorry. You can always call me." She wanted so badly to help, to take away the pain that was still so clearly reflected in his eyes.

He smiled sadly. "Thank you. It's just not the same. You know what I mean."

"I know. But if you're having a rough day, it might help to talk to someone. Even me."

He smiled slightly. "You're right. It probably would."

"How is your dad doing?" Their father was in his mid-seventies and still worked hard at a hobby he loved. He had a machine shop attached to the house and did all kinds of wood-working projects and carvings. Some of them were beautiful pieces of art that he sold at local galleries, and Andrew took some to his Nantucket shop.

"I think he's doing better than I am, actually. He says he joined a local bereavement group and that it helps to focus on his woodworking."

When Lori brought their dinners out, Kristen ordered a second glass of chardonnay. Tyler asked about Chase and Beth's new flipping project and they chatted about that for a bit.

"I always thought it sounded like an interesting thing to do. Until something goes wrong unexpectedly, like their plumbing situation. And at least Chase is a contractor so he can do most of the work himself," Tyler said.

"I know. Those shows never share that some houses don't sell fast enough or end up a loss because of higher expenses. It's way too risky for me. Though it does look fun, when it goes the right way."

Tyler ate every bit of his prime rib and asked for the dessert menu, while Kristen packed up half her pot pie to take home. It was good, just too much and so rich. But she helped Tyler share a dessert. He ordered a special and it was very good—a peanut butter and chocolate ice cream pie with a cookie crust and hot fudge and whipped cream on top.

While he was happily polishing off the dessert and seemed in a somewhat receptive mood, she floated an idea that came to her earlier.

"You mentioned that your father was going to a bereavement group. Maybe you should look into something similar here? It might be good to talk to other people that are going through the same struggle."

As expected, his immediate response was negative. "I think I'm probably too young for that. Isn't it mostly for people who have lost spouses?"

Hm. Maybe it was. "I'm not sure, but you could check. If not a group, maybe a therapist or something? A professional to talk things out?"

"You mean therapy? Yeah, did that once. It didn't help. At all."

Kristen sensed a certain tone in his voice. Tyler was not receptive to the therapy idea or even the bereavement group. She'd drop it for now. But maybe she'd look into it and find out more.

"Aren't you going to finish that?" Tyler glanced at Kristen's glass of wine, which was more than half-full.

"I shouldn't have ordered it. It seemed like a good idea at the time, but once I start eating, I always lose interest in the wine."

Tyler shook his head. "I don't know how you do it. I could never not finish."

When they were done, he insisted on paying the

check, as usual. Sometimes, if Kristen was fast, she could grab the check, and she liked to do that so it wasn't always Tyler paying.

When they arrived home, she assumed that Tyler would invite her in. When he didn't, she asked if he wanted to come over to her place and watch a little TV. She wasn't ready for the night to end and normally after dinner, they would spend more time together.

But Tyler yawned. "I'm really beat. It was a long day today and I'm ready to crash. You don't mind, do you?"

She wanted to scream that yes, she did mind. But that would be selfish.

"No, of course not. Sleep well."

"Actually, do you want to come in for a minute? I have something I want to give to you. I picked it up the other day." He suddenly had a bit more energy, and Kristen was intrigued as she followed him into his cottage.

"I'll be right back." He went into his bedroom, while Kristen waited in the kitchen and glanced around the room. It was a mess. Pizza boxes were on the kitchen counter and coffee table. A bag of trash sat in the corner, waiting to go outside, and mail was piled up on the kitchen island.

When he returned holding a large paper bag, he followed her gaze and made a face.

"I know, it's a mess. I need to call Angela. I canceled her last week because I didn't want to be disturbed. I was having trouble getting into the flow." He handed her the paper bag with a shy grin.

"What's this?"

"You mentioned that you needed some new inspiration and that you wanted to try something different. I was at the Nantucket bookstore browsing, and stumbled onto this and thought of you."

Kristen peeked into the bag and drew out a gorgeous hardcover coffee-table book. It was an oversized collection of stunning Nantucket sunsets. The colors were vivid and the images so breathtaking that goosebumps swept across her arms. The images would be great jumping off points for a whole series of paintings. It was an incredibly thoughtful gift, and she felt her eyes grow damp.

"Thank you. This is incredible."

"I'm glad you like it." He leaned over and touched his lips to hers, and she kissed him back and hoped that maybe he'd changed his mind about wanting an early night. She wanted to keep kissing him. But after a moment, he pulled back and brushed a wayward piece of hair off her face.

"Thanks for coming out tonight. I'll call you tomorrow."

When Kristen left, Tyler locked the door behind her, went into his living room and collapsed on the sofa.

He tried to resist the urge that had grown stronger throughout the evening. For ten more minutes, he resisted as his gaze kept drifting to the polished hardwood hutch and the bottom cabinet. He was simply too unsettled to have invited Kristen in for long—because he knew he was going to satisfy the urge, even as he tried to resist. He knew it was going to win over and if he was honest with himself, he'd been looking forward to it all day and all night. That's why he didn't have the O'Doul's. Because he knew he was coming home to the real thing.

Slowly, he got up and made his way over to the cabinet, opened it and reached way in the back for the slim bottle of Tito's vodka. He chuckled to himself as he saw the label. At least it was gluten-free—not that it mattered. He got his favorite glass from the kitchen, a tall tumbler with an ocean blue bottom that gave the clear liquid a blue tone. He added two ice cubes and then vodka—two thirds of the way up the side of the glass. A splash of soda and a squeeze of lemon and he had the perfect drink.

He took a slow sip and felt an indescribable rush as the cool alcohol slid down his throat. The first drink disappeared quickly. He'd always been a fast drinker, which was part of the problem. He made a second drink and tried to take his time with it. He sipped more slowly as he savored the taste. Vodka was a funny alcohol. It took its time kicking in with any effects, so it was easy to have more than you should, thinking the first drink or two was harmless. But then, it would catch up and hit you all at once.

Tyler was sprawled out on the sofa clicking through TV channels when the buzz hit and a hazy warmth spread through him. It was a delicious sense of well-being. He vaguely knew it was a lie but for the moment, he chose to believe in it. He told himself that he had the drinking under control. That he could stop whenever he wanted and that maybe he'd never really had a problem, he just didn't know how to handle alcohol then. Now, he was older, wiser. And it seemed to help. It dulled the pain and put off the emptiness and the hurt for a little while.

He woke at three in the morning with a pounding headache. He was still on the living room sofa and had a stiff neck from falling asleep in a bad position. The television was blaring an infomercial about a food sealer. Tyler watched, mesmerized, and considered finding his phone and ordering one. But it seemed like too much of an effort, and really what would he do with a food sealer? As he slowly began to wake and to sober up, he realized that wouldn't be smart.

He glanced toward the liquor cabinet and saw that the bottle of vodka that had been nearly three-quarters full was more than half-gone. And his glass on the coffee table was completely empty. He'd had a lot to drink. More than he'd planned. He got up, put the vodka bottle back in its spot, way in the back where it was mostly hidden behind casserole dishes and other things that rarely saw use. So there was little need to open that cabinet.

He rinsed his glass and put it in the dishwasher, then padded into his bedroom and climbed into bed. His last thought before he drifted off to sleep was that he had no other vodka in the house, and the small amount left was not enough.

CHAPTER 12

"You're not hungry today?" Lisa asked Rhett when he got up for a second cup of coffee and didn't make a plate of food. They were sitting at breakfast with Angela and the Mortons, a pleasant couple in their early sixties who were enjoying their first trip to Nantucket. The inn was full but everyone else was still sleeping, so Angela and Lisa were enjoying a leisurely breakfast. Rhett had joined them later than usual. Normally he was the first one in line for coffee, but today he had slept in. When Lisa got up, he was still sound asleep and she didn't want to disturb him.

"I need to wake up a little first. I didn't sleep great last night. Still feel exhausted." He had dark circles under his eyes, and Lisa had noticed that he was getting up more during the night lately.

"Do you feel sick?" She hoped he wasn't coming down with something.

"No, not at all. Just tired. Need a good night's sleep. Hopefully, I'll get it tonight."

"Is everything going okay with the restaurants?" He hadn't mentioned there being any issues, but if there were, it would explain why he wasn't sleeping well.

"Nothing out of the ordinary." Rhett got up and went to get some food. He returned a few minutes later with a plate of fresh cut fruit and one slice of buttered toast. Lisa raised her eyebrows.

"That's all you're having?"

He chuckled as he settled back into his seat and picked up a piece of toast. "Remember I mentioned that I've gained a few pounds? I was serious. They need to come off. I had to go up a notch on my belt, and that hasn't happened in years. I'd like to blame it on your good cooking, but that wouldn't be fair. No one forces me to go back for seconds."

"Hm. Well, we probably could both cut back a little. I've been thinking about trying to eat more plant-based meals and cut back on meat."

Rhett looked alarmed at the thought. "There's no need to go that far."

"It's not what you're thinking. Plant-based is more than a bowl of broccoli. I've been researching it a bit and there are a lot of good, filling recipes."

Rhett still looked skeptical.

"Don't worry, I'll still have plenty of meat options. I

just want to eat more veggies overall. I don't plan to cut anything out entirely, just eat less meat."

"Okay, then."

"We're trying to eat more plant-based, too," Angela said. "Philippe's mother sent us a meal delivery box as a gift a few weeks ago. It had all the ingredients for three meals and they were surprisingly good. Philippe liked them, too. Especially one that was a stuffed sweet potato with quinoa, an herb cheese made from cashews, and a red pepper sauce. It tasted really good and was filling, too. I could send you the recipe if you like?" she offered, and added, "I think even Rhett would like it."

Lisa laughed. "That would be great, thanks. Let me know the name of the meal delivery service, too, that might be an interesting way to try some new recipes."

"I'll send you the info. We liked it so much, we ordered another box."

"How's your cleaning business going? I overheard one of our customers at the bar mention your name the other night," Rhett said.

"I hope it was a good mention?"

"Oh, it was. Someone was looking for a new cleaner and your name was the first one recommended."

Angela smiled. "That's wonderful to hear. I wonder if that was Evelyn Murphy. We got a new client a few days ago. Business is really good."

"Harriet mentioned that you are keeping her busy,"

Lisa said. She was glad to hear it, too, as she'd felt a little guilty that she hadn't been able to hire her back when she returned from being in Jamaica for the winter. But she really needed someone year-round and didn't want to give up her mornings with Angela.

"Yes, she's full-time now and it will work out well because we are definitely going to be slower in the winter when she goes to see her mom in Jamaica."

"Good, that sounds perfect for both of you then."

"Tyler called yesterday, too, and he wants me to start coming weekly again. I'm heading over there this afternoon."

"Oh, I didn't realize he'd stopped." That surprised Lisa.

"He just skipped a week. People do that sometimes. He said he was deep into a book and just didn't want to be disturbed."

"That sounds like Kate. She talks about getting 'into the zone' and how sometimes the story almost writes itself, and other times it's much harder."

"I don't really understand how they do it, but yeah, he said it was something like that. He was really stuck and it was like pulling teeth to get the words…so that's why he didn't want to be interrupted. Would make it even harder, I guess."

"Kristen gets like that, too, with her painting. It must be going well now, as I haven't heard from her in a few days."

Angela smiled. "She had us all over for dinner

recently and mentioned that she'd been having a good week. I was thinking of inviting her and Tyler over for dinner soon, and maybe Kate and Jack, too. All those writers will have plenty to talk about."

"That sounds fun. I'm sure they'd love it," Lisa said as Rhett got up and returned with a generous slice of cheddar and bacon quiche.

He sat back down with a slightly guilty look. "I don't know how anyone can be satisfied with a bowl of fruit for a meal. Dieting is for the birds."

"Dieting is no fun," Lisa agreed. "You don't need to go to extremes, though. Just cut back a little. I know it's easier said than done, but I need to do it, too. I'll try to cook a little healthier this week and do smaller portions. That's my biggest downfall. I always want more."

"Me, too," Rhett agreed.

"And we can make an effort to get more walking in. I was thinking of walking the beach after breakfast. Do you want to join me?"

Rhett grinned after he took the last bite of quiche. He'd inhaled it. "Yes, I will. And I'll resist getting a second serving, even though I really want one."

***

Sue made herself a second cup of coffee and brought it to her kitchen island where her laptop was already fired up. She liked to start her day by going through emails over coffee, then after breakfast, she'd go upstairs to her office and work there for the rest of the day. Often, she'd stay in her pajamas until later in the afternoon, unless she was going somewhere. At some point after lunch, she usually took a break and jumped in the shower and then pulled on a pair of sweatpants and a comfy t-shirt and sweater. She worked better when she was comfortable and it seemed like lately that her waist had expanded a bit, so her jeans felt a little tight. She knew she'd added a few pounds during the past year as she went through menopause— one of several things she didn't like about it, along with hot flashes and feeling more moody than usual. Lisa and Paige had already gone through it and assured her it was all normal and annoying.

Hot coffee often triggered a hot flash, and Sue was sweating profusely as Curt made his way downstairs and into the kitchen for a quick cup before heading into the office. He rarely ate breakfast. He looked sharper than usual this morning. She could definitely see the weight loss. Something else was different, too.

"Is that a new blazer and tie?"

Curt smiled. "Yes. I didn't have a navy one and my others are kind of big, so I picked this up the other day. I saw the tie at Vineyard Vines and thought it was appropriate."

The tie was cute. It was very preppy Nantucket, with pink whales on a turquoise blue background.

"I like it. Brings out the blue in your eyes."

Curt looked pleased and surprised by the compliment.

"Thank you. Are you stopping into the office for the weekly meeting later today?" Every Thursday, they had a weekly meeting at four, where they reviewed the events of the week and made goals for the next week. They often left right after the meeting and went for cocktails at the Club Car. For a few months now, she'd mostly skipped the cocktail hour.

It just didn't interest her the way it used to. She almost always made it in for the meeting, though. That kept her somewhat connected to the ups and downs of the office and she was often able to help with suggestions on how to solve client issues or strategies on how to approach potential new clients.

"I'll be there."

"And drinks after? I think the whole office is going today to celebrate Brad's fourth anniversary." They always liked to make a little fuss on each employee's yearly anniversary with the company. Their employees appreciated the recognition and everyone enjoyed the celebration.

She shook her head. "No, not tonight. I told Lisa and Paige I'd meet them at Millie's for dinner and drinks. But I will order a cake from Stop and Shop and bring it in when I come later today."

"Good. I won't have any, but I know everyone else will love it."

CHAPTER 13

Sue picked up the anniversary cake on her way into the office later that afternoon. The energy in the small office was high when she stepped in the door. Brad was high-fiving Curt and Sue smiled when she saw it, guessing that he had just signed a new policy or a new client.

Curt turned at the sound of the door opening and came over to her.

"Hey, there. Great news, Brad just expanded the Rogers account. They moved all the business and automobile coverage over to us." That was good news. The Rogers were a fairly new account. Brad had met the husband golfing and he'd been looking to lower their home insurance policy. Adding the other coverage meant they were happy with the service they'd received from Brad and the agency. Sue walked over and congratulated him.

"Curt just told me the good news. That's really great to hear, and we have lots to celebrate. It's hard to believe it's your four-year anniversary."

Brad flushed at the compliment.

"Thank you. A good excuse for cake, right?"

Sue smiled. "Yes, and you might need to have Curt's share, too, since he's off carbs."

Brad laughed. "That won't be a problem."

Sue set the cake in the conference room and everyone in the office gathered there promptly at four. Curt led the meeting and everyone shared their wins and challenges for the week.

Brandi had a challenge with a client that was considering dropping them to go with a less expensive option, and Sue gave her some data and walked her through an approach that could hopefully save the account, to show how a slightly more expensive policy with better coverage could save the client money in the long run. Brandi took detailed notes and looked grateful.

"Thank you. The detailed numbers info might do it with them. They are so focused on the data."

When they finished up, Curt asked Sue again if she wanted to join them for drinks.

"Come with us," Brandi chimed in. "It's been ages since you've come out."

Sue was surprised somewhat by the comment and flattered, too. It was nice to be wanted.

"Thanks. I will soon, but I can't tonight, I have

another commitment. You guys have fun, though. You all deserve it. You're all doing a great job." A few minutes later, as she grabbed her coat and purse and turned to leave, Sue noticed that Brandi and Curt were deep in conversation. Brandi was smiling and Curt was leaning toward her, totally engrossed in what she was saying. Neither one of them looked her way as Sue opened the front door.

WHEN SUE REACHED MILLIE'S RESTAURANT, SHE SAW Lisa's car parked by the door. She went upstairs, and both Lisa and Paige were already sitting at a table, sipping margaritas. Sue glanced at her watch and it was only a few minutes past six.

"We both got here a little early and saw a margarita go by, so we went ahead and ordered drinks," Lisa said with a smile as Sue shrugged her coat off and settled into a chair. A moment later, their waitress came by and Sue ordered a margarita as well. As soon as it arrived, they all tapped their glasses together and toasted to a night out.

"What's Curt up to tonight?" Paige asked.

"He went for after-work drinks with a few others in the office. One of the guys work anniversary is today and they usually go for drinks after the weekly meeting, anyway. Just an excuse to celebrate."

"Cheers to that." Lisa lifted her glass and took a sip.

"You didn't want to go out with them? We could have rescheduled," Paige said.

Sue smiled. "No, I'd much rather be out with you two."

"Is Brandi going with them?" Lisa asked.

"Yes, she asked if I was going to join them. Said I hadn't been out with them in ages. I haven't. I probably should go one of these weeks."

Paige looked thoughtful. "I would. She's a pretty girl. I wouldn't want her spending too much time with my husband. If I was married."

The image of Brandi and Curt deep in thought as Sue left came to her for a moment and she shook it off.

"I'm not worried about Brandi, or Curt. He's a harmless flirt."

"True. But he's lost quite a bit of weight, you said? He's a handsome guy. And she's single. Might not be a bad idea to just remind her that you two have a great relationship," Paige said.

"I've never had to worry about Curt," Sue said without hesitation.

"No. But how well do you know this Brandi? She's the one I'd maybe be a little concerned about." Paige took the last sip of her margarita and looked around to catch the waitress's attention to order another.

"Things are good with you and Curt, right?" Lisa asked.

The question took Sue by surprise.

"Yes, things are fine. Totally fine." She'd never had to worry about Curt before.

"I'm sure it's nothing." Paige smiled as the waitress came over and she ordered a second drink, and a platter of loaded nachos and side of guacamole and chips for the table.

"What's nothing?" Sue was confused by Paige's tone.

"Remember what I mentioned to you on the phone?" Lisa asked.

Paige leaned in and lowered her voice. "Lisa and I saw Curt and Brandi and a few others at the Club Car. Brandi was very friendly and kind of touchy feely with Curt, hand on his arm, that kind of thing. But it really probably is nothing. Don't give it another thought."

Sue thought about that, and also knew that Paige was extra sensitive to this kind of thing, as two long-term relationships had ended when she'd caught her partners cheating. She suspected she was seeing something that wasn't really there.

"I won't. So, what else is new with you two?"

"Miriam Carlton just filed for divorce. I ran into her at the market yesterday," Lisa said.

Sue's jaw dropped. "Miriam, really? I thought she and Ryan had the perfect marriage. What happened?"

Lisa hesitated for a moment. "We went for coffee and she told me everything. I think she needed to talk. He cheated with his secretary."

"Such a cliche." Paige shook her head in disgust.

"They always looked so happy," Sue said. "And they have kids, too? Twins?"

"Yeah. Melissa and Cody are juniors in high school now. Miriam blamed him, of course, but she also said that they'd grown apart. She was a stay-at-home mother while he mostly worked all week in Boston or New York and flew home on the weekends. He worked most weekends, too, and they stopped doing things together as much as they used to. It still took her by surprise, though."

"That's too bad. How did she find out?"

"He was in the shower and his phone went nuts. Kept buzzing with text messages. It was so urgent that she glanced at the phone to see if it was some kind of emergency. That's when she saw that it was Karli, his secretary, but the messages were not at all work related."

"What did she do?" Paige smiled as the waitress set down her margarita.

"She said she sat there in shock, but when her husband came out of the bathroom, she handed him his phone and asked him what was going on. There was no way he could explain the messages, so he confessed. He begged her to stay, said it was a momentary lapse that didn't mean anything, but she wasn't having any of it."

"Did she consider staying with him?" Sue asked.

"She said she did for about two seconds. But the more she thought about it, the more she was convinced that Karli wasn't his first. Other things that she'd dismissed before took on new meaning. But, more than anything, she said she simply could never trust him again," Lisa said.

"The first time is the hardest. Once they open that door and get away with it, the temptation can be hard to resist. Remember when I gave Bob a second chance? That didn't last long." Paige said.

Sue did remember. Paige and Bob were engaged and had been together for almost eight years. A few months before the wedding, she discovered he'd been unfaithful. He swore it was just a one-off, that it didn't mean anything. And she loved him, so she took him at his word. But things were never the same again. She ended it and learned that it hadn't actually been the first time he cheated. It was just the first time he got caught.

So now, after Lisa's conversation with Miriam, Sue understood why they'd asked about Curt and Brandi. But, she knew Curt and trusted him implicitly. Still, it probably wouldn't be a bad idea to be more social with everyone in the office. Next time they all went out, she'd join them, even if it was just for one drink. Curt could stay out all night and Sue just didn't enjoy that anymore, being the last ones left at the bar. No, she'd make an appearance, then head home, get comfy in her pajamas and curl up in front of the TV or with a good book.

CHAPTER 14

C hase did most of the work on the flip house on weekends, so that it wouldn't cut too much into his other contracted work. Since they'd met with Rick, he'd taken care of the plumbing issues and had moved on to the renovation work. Beth knew Chase was worried about the overall costs, though, and she was, too. Neither of them could afford to take a loss on the project.

She'd told Chase she'd stop in mid-day once she had all the samples and they could look at them together in the house and decide which tiles, backsplash and flooring to go with. She had a good selection of options, but she had her favorites that she thought could make the most impact—now she just had to persuade Chase that the slightly more expensive options might be the most cost-effective in the long run, when it resulted in a higher price.

She gathered up all the samples in a big cardboard box, put them in the back seat of her Honda Civic, and drove out to the house. She could hear the sound of a power saw as she opened the front door. Chase didn't even turn until she got closer and set her box on the kitchen counter. He turned off the saw and stood, brushing wood dust off his work jeans.

"Hey, there. Are these all the samples?"

"Yes, let me know what you think." Beth laid all the tile samples on the counter and the wood samples on the floor. Once they saw the pieces on the floor, two looked really good.

"These two cost about the same." She liked both equally.

"Okay, let's do this one, then." Chase pointed to the lighter of the two options and she made a note on her phone and then put them back in the box.

Beth had grouped the tiles by color combinations, varying shades of blue and gray with ivory and cream. Chase immediately pointed to her favorite combination, an elegant gray with a hint of blue and a creamy white.

"I like that one, but what's the cost of the different options?"

Beth told him, and he frowned when he realized the one he liked was the most expensive.

"Maybe we should go with this one instead." He pointed to the least expensive option, which also the most ordinary.

"That one is my least favorite. And remember what you said. An upscale look will sell better. We'll be able to get a higher price. It should pay off more, even though it's slightly more expensive now."

"We can't afford it. Go with the cheaper one." He bent over to turn his saw back on and Beth glared at him.

"No. We need to discuss this. I don't want the cheaper one, and you don't either. You just don't want to spend the money."

"Beth, we don't have the money to spend. Be reasonable." The irritation in his voice was evident. But Beth wasn't backing down.

"I know to the penny what we have to spend. We can do the ones we want, we just can't have any more unplanned expenses."

"And you can guarantee that we won't?" he snapped.

She took a step back. Chase had never spoken to her like that before.

"Of course I can't guarantee that. But at this point, what could still crop up as an expected expense? We've already done the big stuff with the plumbing, and you've checked everything else. Aside from the cosmetic stuff you're doing now, there's nothing else left, right?"

"Right."

"So, tell me again why we can't do the combination that we both want? That we know will look the best and get us the highest price?"

Chase sighed. "Fine, Beth. We'll go with the ones you want. Are you happy now?"

"Am I happy? I've been better. I think I'm going to go visit my mother this afternoon and will spend the night there. So I'll talk to you tomorrow and hopefully you'll be in a better mood."

"I'm in a fine mood," Chase muttered.

"Right. Well, enjoy your fine mood and I'll talk to you later." Beth gathered up her box of samples and headed to her car, walking quickly before the tears came. Chase had never spoken to her like that, and she realized that they'd had their first fight. It had taken her by surprise and while she knew that he was just stressed about money, it still hurt because she had the same worries.

WHEN CHASE'S IRRITATION FADED, IT WAS REPLACED BY feelings of guilt. He knew he'd upset Beth. He'd never been angry with her before, and the look of hurt on her face pained him to see. To know he'd hurt her. But still, she could be so stubborn sometimes, and he'd known she wasn't going to give up about those tiles. Her persistence was something he'd always admired about her, while at the same time it could also be frustrating.

But, she was also right. There really shouldn't be any other unexpected expenses popping up at this point. And he had been the one who said upscale was the way to go. They just both had a lot of money tied up in this project, and he wanted to protect what they'd invested. But the design combination they both liked was the one that would sell better. There was no doubt about that.

Chase sighed. He knew he owed Beth an apology. His first inclination was to call immediately and ask her not to spend the night at her mother's, to come home to him instead. But then he realized that it might be good for them to have a short break, for both of them to calm down.

So, he texted her. "Sorry I was a grump. Tell your mom I said hi, and I'll talk to you tomorrow."

A few seconds later, her reply flashed back, 'ok.'

He knew she was still upset. He'd apologize thoroughly tomorrow and see if she wanted to go out to dinner. He didn't think Beth would stay upset for long —although this was their first argument, so he didn't know that for sure.

CHAPTER 15

Kristen was looking forward to going to Angela and Philippe's house for dinner. Kate and Jack were going, too, and all the guys got along well. Angela had said not to bother making anything, but Kristen didn't want to show up empty-handed so she baked some chocolate chip cookies and had a bottle of Pinot Noir to bring over.

The plan was for Tyler to drive since he didn't drink, and Kristen was going to walk over to his cottage at a quarter of six. She was all dressed and ready to head out the door when her cell rang, and it was Tyler.

"I'm just heading over now. I'll be there in a sec."

There was an uncomfortably long silence before Tyler finally said, "I don't think I can make it tonight."

"What? Why not? Are you sick?" He'd sounded fine when she checked in with him earlier in the day.

"Yeah, I'm feeling lousy. I think I'm coming down with something. I don't want to get anyone else sick."

"Are you sure? I'm sorry you're not feeling well. We don't have to stay out late, though." Kristen couldn't hide her disappointment.

Tyler hesitated for a moment. "No, I think it's best if I skip this one. You go and have fun. I'm sure it will be a good time."

"Okay. You will be missed, though. Feel better."

"Thanks."

TWENTY MINUTES LATER, SHE PULLED UP TO ANGELA and Philippe's house. Kate and Jack's car was already outside. Angela answered the door, pulled her in for a quick hug and looked behind her for Tyler.

"Tyler couldn't make it. He's sick."

"Oh, no! I'm sorry to hear that."

"Yeah, it seems to have come on suddenly. He was fine earlier. Anyway, here are cookies for dessert and my new favorite red wine." She handed Angela the plate of cookies.

"You didn't have to bring anything, but thank you. Did you make these?"

Kristen nodded. "It's the same ones I made when you came over."

"Oh, good. Come on in. Jack and Kate are already here."

Kristen followed Angela into the kitchen where

everyone was gathered around the big island. Crackers and cheese and a bowl of nuts were already out, and everyone was nibbling.

"Should we open this?" Angela asked. "Kate and I were just trying to decide whether we want white or red."

"Yes, let's open it. I don't think Kate has tried this one yet."

"Is Tyler coming?" Philippe asked after pulling Kristen in for a welcome hug.

She shook her head. "No. He's sorry to miss it. He's sick."

"Oh, that's too bad," Kate said as Angela handed her a glass of wine. She took a sip and Kristen could tell she liked it. "What kind of wine is this?" she asked Angela.

"Your sister brought it."

"It's that pinot I told you about, Charles Krug. I thought you'd like it."

"Love it."

"I invited Abby and Jeff, too, but Abby called earlier and said the baby is sick, so they didn't want to leave her," Angela said. "It doesn't sound like it's anything serious but she had a slight fever."

"Oh, poor Natalie," Kate said. "Maybe that's what Tyler has, too? Could be something is going around."

They chatted for a while in the kitchen, snacking and sipping wine. Philippe put out some fresh shrimp with a spicy cocktail sauce, too.

Philippe was in charge of the main course—marinated swordfish on the outside grill, while Angela had a few side dishes going on the stove. When everything was ready, they sat down to eat in the dining room. The swordfish was cooked perfectly and was delicious. Angela's whipped potatoes were light and fluffy, and the roasted asparagus went well with it.

Conversation was lively over dinner and as usual, it turned to writing. Philippe gave updates on where he was with his current project, a novel this time.

"I have to admit, I'm kind of glad to take a break from the TV stuff. It's nice to just be here on the island, sitting in my office every morning, staring out at the waves. Doesn't get any better than that."

"When do you have to head back out West?" Jack asked as he reached for more potatoes.

"Not until the fall. Thankfully." Philippe turned his attention to Kate. "I don't suppose you've heard any updates on your movie option?"

Kate's first book had attracted the attention of a brother-sister team that she'd met through Philippe. Her first freelance project after leaving the magazine had been to interview Philippe, as he was active with the Nantucket Film Festival.

"I actually heard from them last week. They warned me that it might take a while. They are waiting to hear back from their development contacts. I'm glad you warned me not to get too excited."

"Unfortunately, actually getting the movie made is

the exception, not the rule. Lots of projects are optioned, sometimes more than once. One of my books had three different production companies option it."

"Was it ever made?" Kristen asked.

Philippe laughed. "Nope. The last option expired six months ago and they didn't renew it. I'm not giving up hope, though. You never know."

"How's Tyler's book coming along?" Kate asked Kristen.

"Good, I think. He said he's further in now and it's starting to come together."

Angela glanced her way and smiled. "Do you have any shows coming up soon?" It reminded Kristen that she had a few phone calls she needed to make the next day.

"I need to call Andrew, now that you mention it. He told me to let him know when I was ready to do another show and I have a few new paintings that might be good."

"Well, let us know when you schedule it."

"I will, thanks."

WHEN THEY FINISHED EATING, ANGELA INSISTED THAT everyone go into the living room while she cleaned up. Kristen and Kate helped her carry the dishes to the sink, and Angela shooed them away.

"It will just take me a few minutes to load the dishwasher. Do you want to set out your cookies?"

Kristen did as instructed and brought the cookies into the living room. Philippe and Jack pounced on them and Kate laughed.

"You'd never know the two of you said you were stuffed just a few minutes ago."

"There's always room for dessert." Philippe grinned as he reached for a second cookie.

Kate took one too and offered the plate to Kristen, but she shook her head.

"I really am too full. Plus, I may have had one or two this afternoon while I was making them."

Angela joined them and asked if anyone wanted coffee. Kristen would have preferred a glass of wine, but she'd already had two so she knew coffee was a wiser option since Tyler wasn't there to drive.

Philippe turned on a basketball game, and he and Jeff turned their attention to it. Angela made a face at the TV.

"I think basketball is the most boring game. You only need to watch the last two minutes. Let's go into the kitchen so we can chat."

They followed her and settled around the island, sipping coffee and catching up on all the local gossip.

"Any more new clients?" Kristen asked Angela. She was impressed by how Angela's business had grown.

"Yes, actually. Brandi from Sue's insurance agency.

I think she's around your age. Did you go to school with her?"

Kate shook her head. "No, she's not local. I remember Mom said she moved here specifically to work at their agency. I think they used a headhunter to find her."

"It can be hard to find experienced people here, unless it's restaurant or tourist related work," Kristen explained.

"Her condo is gorgeous," Angela said. "It's right down by the pier, and it's all soft pinks, blues and grays and lots of white."

"Does she live by herself?" Kristen was curious.

Angela nodded. "Yeah, with her white Himalayan cat, Gidget. She's a beauty." Two seconds later, almost as if she'd called his name, Angela's cat Sam strolled into the room and rubbed against her leg. She reached down and scratched him behind his ears. "Yes, you're a beauty, too."

"I can't imagine moving here not knowing anyone. I wonder how she's liking it so far?" Kristen said.

Angela laughed. "That's pretty much what I did. I didn't know a soul when I first got here."

"Well, you weren't planning to stay either, though," Kristen reminded her.

"That's true, and I was lucky to sit next to your mom on the plane ride here, and then to meet all of you."

"And Philippe, too," Kate said. "There really is

something to that old saying that love finds you when you're not looking for it."

"It's very true," Kristen agreed.

"It can be hard to meet people here, especially in the winter when it's so much quieter," Kate sipped her coffee and looked around the room.

"I like the changes you've made." Philippe's house was gorgeous. Kate had visited before when she was interviewing him and they became friends. The house had a masculine feel at the time, but Angela had added candles and soft throws here and there, and now it was just beautiful and homey.

"Thank you. I wanted to give it a bit of my touch, adding things that I loved, and now it feels more like our home, instead of just Philippe's."

Kristen thought about how different her cottage was from Tyler's, although they were identical in size and layout. His had a darker, more masculine feel. She wondered how he was doing, and if he was feeling better.

"Before I forget, there were a lot of leftovers so I made a plate for Tyler if you want to take it to him. When he feels like eating, he'll have a good homemade meal he can just heat up," Angela said.

"Oh, that was nice of you. I was just thinking about him. If his lights are on, I'll drop it off on my way home."

.   .   .

AN HOUR LATER, AFTER EVERYONE HAD SAID THEIR goodbyes and headed home, Kristen pulled into her driveway. It was just a few minutes past ten, and Tyler's lights were all still on. She grabbed the container Angela had packed and walked the short distance to his house.

When she reached the door, she knocked and waited a few minutes. Then knocked again. She heard footsteps finally and then a loud crash, a few swear words, and finally the door opened.

Tyler stood there in bare feet, sweatpants and an old, faded Red Sox t-shirt. His hair was mussed and his eyes were heavy. He looked horrible. She looked beyond him and saw a table where he kept pots and pans was on its side and two pans on the floor. She guessed he must have just knocked them over on his way to open the door.

"I'm sorry. I hope I didn't wake you? I saw the lights were on and wanted to give you this. Angela sent me home with a plate of food for you. The swordfish was really good. I'll just put it in the fridge and you can heat it up tomorrow."

Tyler just nodded sleepily as she quickly walked to the kitchen and put the container on the top shelf. She noticed that there was nothing in the fridge except for a few limes and some soda water, so it was a good thing Angela had sent the food home.

When she closed the refrigerator and turned around, her eyes fell on the cutting board by the sink where there was a sliced lime and next to that, a half-empty bottle of vodka. Her spirits sank as Tyler's recent behavior began to make sense. She turned to face him. He was leaning on his kitchen island, watching her, and looked like he was trying to focus.

"You weren't sick tonight, were you?"

He looked down and away before mumbling, "No, not exactly." When he spoke, waves of alcohol fumes poured off him. Kristen wasn't sure what to do. This was a situation that was foreign to her. Without thinking too much about it, she grabbed the bottle of vodka and poured it down the sink.

Tyler flinched as it disappeared down the drain.

"Did you have to do that?"

She knew that to him, it was a shocking waste of good alcohol. Too bad.

"Tyler, let's get you to bed. We'll talk tomorrow. For now, you need to sleep."

His eyes were already half shut as he swayed by the island. She took his arm and led him to his bedroom, and he went with no protest. Once they reached his bed, she waited for him to climb in and folded his covers over him like one would do for a small child. Meanwhile, Kristen's emotions were all over the place, ranging from furious to numb to heartbreakingly sad.

She turned off his lights and closed the door behind her as she went back to the kitchen and straightened out the pots and pans, putting them back in their spots. She threw out the cut limes and put the knife and cutting board in his dishwasher, and the empty bottle of vodka in the trash.

When she left, she locked the door behind her. As she walked home to her cottage, the tears that had threatened to come spilled over. She had no experience with this and didn't know what it meant. What had caused Tyler to relapse? Was there something she could have done to prevent it?

Did it mean that their relationship wasn't strong enough to keep him from drinking? That was the most confusing thing of all. What did this mean for their relationship? She fell into bed and tossed and turned for a long time before settling on a plan to call Tyler's brother, Andrew, in the morning. He would know what to do.

CHAPTER 16

Tyler woke the next morning in a world of pain. The sun streaming through his window was so bright and his head was throbbing. It felt like a bunch of tiny men with ice picks were hammering away. His mouth was dry and when he rolled over, his stomach heaved. He gave his odds of making it to the bathroom in time at about fifty-fifty.

He barely made it there and spent the next five minutes with his arms wrapped around the toilet. When there was nothing left but dry heaves, he slowly pulled himself up, swallowed a few Ibuprofen, washed his face and felt like the walking dead as he trudged to the kitchen and found his cell phone on the counter. There were two messages, one from Kristen and one from Andrew, about ten minutes apart.

He grabbed a bottle of cold water and popped a K-cup in the coffeemaker. Coffee would help the headache, too. Once it was brewed, he brought the steaming mug and his water to the living room where he collapsed on the sofa, took a sip of the hot coffee and stared at his phone. He assumed that Kristen had called Andrew. He didn't blame her.

His memory of the night before was hazy, but he remembered enough to know that his little secret was out. Kristen had seen him at his worst, and he was sorry for that. But he also felt a sense of relief. It was too hard keeping that secret, trying to hide the drinking. He listened to Kristen's message first.

"Hi, Tyler. I'm guessing that you probably aren't feeling so great this morning. I'm sorry about that. I...I called Andrew. I'm sorry about that, too, but I know he'd want to know. We both want to help you to get the help you need. Andrew is coming here at noon, and then we're both coming to see you. We can get through this."

Tyler smiled at the nervous optimism in her voice. He hoped that she was right. Andrew's message basically said the same thing, that they'd be by around noon to make a plan. He knew they both meant well and were worried for him. But he knew what he needed to do. It had worked before.

He picked up the phone and called Scotty, his sponsor. Scotty wouldn't be surprised to hear his news as Tyler hadn't been at a meeting in over a week. Scotty had left two messages and sounded worried, and Tyler had finally called him back yesterday and lied, said he was out of town. Scotty answered on the first ring.

"You're not out of town, are you?"

"No, sorry about that." Tyler paused for a moment. "What's the name of that place you mentioned to me once? Miller something, on the Cape?"

"Murphy House in Falmouth. If you want to make the call, I'll take you there. I've been needing to get off-island, anyway."

"You sure? I could probably get my brother to go with me."

"I'm sure. We'll take the slow boat, so I can bring the truck and it will be good. We'll get some coffee and settle in for a good talk."

"Thanks, Scotty. I'll make the call, and I'll book the tickets for the boat, too."

He googled the phone number of Murphy House, and it didn't take long to confirm a spot. He felt a sense of relief when he ended the call. It was a little past ten. He had two hours before Kristen and Andrew would arrive. Tyler closed his eyes for just a minute…and woke to the sound of loud knocking on the door. He stretched slowly and glanced at the time on his cell phone. Somehow, it was already ten past noon.

He eased off the sofa and took a deep breath. His head was pounding a little less now, but it still hurt. His whole body felt like one big bruise and he really wanted a drink. Kristen had been smart to pour out the last of the vodka. He would have reached for it instead of coffee if it had been an option. It would have made him feel better, temporarily. What they said about the hair of the dog was true. He didn't really want a drink. It was just his body that did, but it was hard to say no. His body was persuasive.

He opened the front door and Kristen and Andrew were standing there wearing identical worried expressions. He didn't quite know what to say, so he just waved them in and walked toward the kitchen.

"Coffee? Water? I don't have much else to offer you."

"No, thanks. I already had coffee," Kristen said.

"I'm all set."

"So, where do you want to do this?" Tyler looked around the living room. "We can get comfortable on the sofa."

"That's fine." Kristen settled on the smaller of the two sofas, and Andrew sat on one corner of the big sofa. Tyler sat on the opposite corner and took another deep breath. He wanted to tell them not to worry, that it would all be fine. But the words wouldn't come right away. He was embarrassed that he'd failed both of them. Failed himself.

"It's been a hard time for both of us," Andrew began. "I'm sorry that I didn't see that you were really struggling." Tyler saw the guilt in his eyes and stomped it out.

"Not your fault, at all. Yes, I've been struggling. But I made the decision to drink again. I stopped going to meetings. Started plotting how I would do it and then I put the plan into motion. I had a delivery service bring groceries and a bottle of vodka." He met Kristen's eyes and tried to explain.

"I looked forward all day to that first drink. That's why I didn't have an O'Doul's when we went out."

"And that's why you didn't want me to come in. You couldn't wait to have a drink."

"Drinks," he corrected her. "And yeah, I'm not proud of it. It's why I didn't go to the dinner last night. I would have been too antsy with everyone drinking. When I'm really sober, I can handle it. I just knew I couldn't do it. And I had my own party here."

"So, what will you do now? Will you start going to meetings again? What can we do to help?" Andrew asked.

"Scotty told me about a place on the Cape that I can go to for a little while, a few weeks or so."

"A treatment program?" Andrew looked hopeful.

"Yeah. I think it's the best thing. It will help to be away from temptation until I can get myself sorted. It helped before."

"I think it's a great idea. Can you have visitors there?" Kristen sounded relieved and apprehensive. Tyler knew she'd never experienced anything like this before.

"Yeah, I think on the weekend they have visiting hours in the afternoon, maybe." He thought the woman he'd talked to had mentioned something about that.

"Good. I'll come visit then."

Her sweet, caring smile was like a beacon of hope. Kristen was the best thing in his life. That she hadn't already walked away was nothing short of a miracle. He looked at both of them and felt so many emotions.

"I'm so sorry, you guys. I really messed up." He sighed and looked down, trying to gather himself so that he wouldn't dissolve in tears. He felt arms around him, hugging him close. Andrew gave him a squeeze, then let go and looked him in the eyes.

"This isn't your fault. I know you didn't want this to happen. You'd been doing so well. Mom dying so unexpectedly—well, it was hard. I know that."

Tyler nodded. "It was the beginning of a spiral down. It was hard to write, hard to focus. I got behind and that added to the stress. It started to seem like a good idea. I fought it as long as I could."

"You can fight it again. And we'll be here for you when you come back. When do you go?" Kristen asked.

"This afternoon."

She looked surprised. "So soon."

"How will you get there? I can find someone to cover the shop, or just close it. I can take you," Andrew insisted.

"Scotty's going to take me. Said he needed to go

off-cape, anyway. I don't think he really did, but it will be good for us to just talk about stuff."

Andrew relaxed. "Okay, good. Scotty's probably familiar with that place, too."

"Yeah. He hasn't been there himself, but he's been to places like it. I think it might be good for him, too, to go there with me and then to go home. A reminder of sorts, maybe."

"Okay. Well, I'm glad we have a good plan then. I'm going to let you guys talk a bit. Call me when you're settled in. I'll get over to visit while you're there, too." Andrew gave him a hug goodbye and left.

When the door shut behind him, Kristen walked over and sat next to him. She pulled him in for a hug. He held her tight and breathed in the sweet apple scent of her hair. He was going to miss her.

"I'm sorry," he said again. "I know you didn't really sign up for this."

She took hold of his hands and squeezed them gently.

"I did, though. It was always in the back of my mind. What would I do if you relapsed? Now I know. I'm sorry you have to go through this. I can't begin to understand it, but I know it's not something you can always control. It's a disease." Her eyes were sad as she looked at him.

"I really was doing so well. This was my first and will hopefully be my last relapse. I just need to get my head in the right place again. I think it will help to talk to someone. Andrew had suggested I go see someone when we got back from the funeral, but I didn't think I needed it. Thought I could just handle it on my own. I was wrong. It just made me crave the release of a drink. It's hard to explain. But I just wanted to forget and to numb the pain."

"I think I understand. How long will you be gone?"

"Almost a month. It's a twenty-eight-day program."

"What will it be like there? Did you look it up online?"

"I did. It looks nice enough. It's a big house, and it's all guys. I saw something about basketball and a few other sports, yoga even. Lots of fresh air, exercise and group sessions to talk stuff out."

"That sounds good. Can you bring your laptop, too?"

"They said I could. It's a structured day, but we get a few free hours in there, so I'll be able to get some writing in, hopefully."

As horrible as he felt about having let everyone down, he was also looking forward to going, he realized. The idea of having everything planned, a daily routine that he just had to follow along, was appealing. It was a break of sorts, from everything. And as much as he would miss Kristen, he wasn't going to miss hiding his drinking from her. To think that he chose to have a drink over spending more time with her—he was deeply ashamed of that. And grateful that she hadn't run screaming. He needed to get himself together, get back on track for himself. And for her, too.

"Well, if there's anything you need. Anything I can do to help, just let me know."

"Thank you. I promise you, I'll be better after this."

She pulled him in and gave him a sweet kiss goodbye.

"I know you will. And I'll see you next weekend."

CHAPTER 17

Rhett had jokingly warned Lisa that he snored when he moved in with her, but she had assured him that she was a sound sleeper so it wasn't likely to be an issue. And it wasn't. But what did get Lisa's attention one night when she'd woken to use the bathroom and then climbed back into bed was how the snoring and Rhett's breathing suddenly stopped. She was alarmed and was about to shake him awake when he started breathing again. He did it a few more times before she fell asleep again, and over coffee the next morning she asked him about it.

"Do you know that you stop breathing sometimes when you sleep?"

They were alone in the dining room. No one else had arrived yet for breakfast. Angela would be there any minute, and Kristen had texted her that she was stopping by for breakfast, too, which was a treat. Lisa always loved it when the girls dropped by and she hadn't had a good chat with Kristen for a few weeks.

Rhett paused before taking another sip. "What are you talking about?"

"I woke in the middle of the night to use the bathroom and you were snoring as usual, but then you stopped snoring and breathing. I almost nudged you, but then you started up again. It wasn't a one-time thing. You did it several more times that I was aware of."

"Hm. Are you sure? That's the first time I've ever heard that."

"I know what I didn't hear. You breathing. Maybe it's sleep apnea. You should call your doctor."

Rhett made a face. "Isn't that where people wear masks?"

Lisa shot him a stern look. "Yes, but it saves their lives. Sleep apnea is a serious condition, from the little I know. Your doctor will probably order a sleep study and then you'll know."

Another thought occurred to her. "You know you have been complaining about being really tired lately. Maybe there's a connection."

"Hm. Okay, I'll call my doctor."

A FEW MINUTES LATER, ANGELA AND KRISTEN WALKED in together along with Edith and Tom Henry, who had just checked in the day before. Lisa walked over to greet the Henrys.

"Help yourself to whatever you'd like. There's cereal and bagels and fruit on the side bar, along with coffee, tea and juice. And today's hot dish is a spinach and tomato frittata with white cheddar."

When she returned to the table where she and Rhett had been sitting, he stood to leave.

"I'm heading out. Have a lot to do today." He winked at her. "And an appointment to make."

She smiled and gave him a quick kiss before sending him on his way. "Have a great day. Don't forget, we have dinner tonight with Sue and Curt."

"Oh, right. I'll be back by then."

She watched him go with a smile before sitting down and joining the girls, who were both eating a slice of the frittata. Angela always had a good appetite, but it surprised her to see Kristen eating something other than fruit.

"This is really good," Kristen said. "I woke up starving today. Forgot to eat dinner last night."

Lisa shook her head. "Thanks, honey. It always amazes me when you don't think to stop to eat. That would never in a million years happen to me."

Angela laughed. "Me, too. I'm always thinking about what I'm going to eat next. Okay, now that I've said that out loud it doesn't sound very healthy, does it?"

"Oh, I'm the same way," Lisa said. "So, what's new with the two of you?"

"Nothing new for me. Just crazy busy with work, which is a good thing."

Lisa smiled. "That is a very good thing."

Kristen took the last bite of her frittata and set her food down.

"Well, I have something to share. Tyler relapsed. He left yesterday afternoon for a rehab in Falmouth."

"Oh, honey, I'm so sorry. Is he okay?"

"He will be. It sounds like it's a nice place. He seemed to think it will help. He went through a similar program once."

"How long will he be there?" Angela asked.

"Almost a month, I guess. They have visiting hours on the weekends, so I'll head over and see how he's doing on Saturday."

"What caused him to relapse? Do you know?" Lisa knew his mother's death had hit him hard. Her heart went out to him. She worried for Kristen, too. She knew that she would want to be there to support Tyler. But what if this wasn't a one-time thing?

"He's been really struggling with losing his mother. I think the stress of that on top of moving here and starting over after his divorce. His wife couldn't take it anymore."

"A friend of mine dated an alcoholic. They were engaged, actually, but she ended up calling it off. It got to her after a while. Her fiancé was always struggling. Falling off the wagon, then promising it would never happen again. And then it did."

Kristen looked horrified before getting up for more coffee. Angela caught a glimpse of her expression and seemed to realize she'd said the wrong thing.

"I'm sure it's very different with Tyler. Forget I even said that."

Kristen sat back down with a full-to-the-rim mug of steaming coffee.

"No, don't worry about it. To be honest, I have wondered about that. It's my biggest fear. Will this keep happening? And can I handle it if it does?"

"I'm sure it will be fine. If it happens again, you'll see the signs and be able to help."

"I hope so. I want to be able to support him. I hope he likes it at this place and that it helps him."

"Have you looked into joining an Al-Anon group?" Lisa suggested. "That might help, and you will need the support, too, especially when he first comes home." This was what Lisa had worried about when she first met Tyler and realized he and Kristen were getting serious. She liked him quite a bit, but she worried for both of them.

"I did visit a local group a while back, just to learn more. Looks like I may need to start going more often.

I think you may be right about the support. I've read about this, but I haven't experienced it before."

"I think that should help. And, of course, I'll do whatever I can. Just let me know how I can help," Lisa said.

Kristen smiled and her eyes looked suspiciously damp. Lisa couldn't help noticing the dark circles under her daughter's eyes. She recognized stress when she saw it.

"Thanks. Just listening is the best thing you can do."

"I can do better than that. Come for Sunday dinner. I'll make your favorite comfort food—home-made gnocchi with gorgonzola cream sauce and prosciutto." Lisa hadn't made it in ages because it was so rich, but Kristen didn't have to worry about calories. She could use more of them. Unlike Lisa, who was a stress eater, Kristen tended to avoid eating when she was highly stressed. So, Lisa would make a big batch and send Kristen home with a big container full of left-over gnocchi.

Her eyes lit up. "Oh, yum. That would be wonderful."

Lisa invited Angela to join them as well. "You and Philippe are welcome, too. There will be plenty of food."

But Angela regretfully declined. "That sounds amazing, but we have another commitment. Some friends of Philippe's invited us over."

Kristen stood and picked up her plate to bring to the kitchen. "I have to run, but thank you for breakfast and I will see you tomorrow. I'll bring some wine."

Lisa stood and gave her a hug. "Take care of yourself, honey. Don't hesitate to call if you need anything."

CHAPTER 18

"Where are you off to now?" Sue smiled as her daughter Stephanie, who lived in Monterey, California, told her that she was calling to let her know she'd be out of the country for the next week. Stephanie was a traveling nurse and fell in love with the West Coast on one of her assignments. She was thirty-five, single, and loved to travel.

"I'm doing a ten-day tour through Italy and France. It's a cooking tour, so we'll be making pasta and drinking wine in Tuscany."

"That sounds fabulous." Sue had never been to Italy.

"Do you and Dad have any trips planned? It's been ages since you went anywhere." She had a good point. It had been a very long time since she and Curt had gone away together for more than a night or two.

"No, nothing planned. But you're right. It has been

too long. Maybe I will investigate one of these tours. I'll wait to get the full report from you when you return."

"Okay, sounds good. I'll call you when I'm back. Give my love to Dad, too."

Sue hung up the phone and thought about what her daughter had said. Eating her way through Italy did sound wonderful. And she and Curt were long overdue for a trip. He'd suggested a vacation several times over the past year or two, and each time, she'd put it off. They were always so busy with work, it seemed.

Curt was off at work in the morning and then off to another committee meeting this afternoon. She'd reminded him that Lisa and Rhett were coming for dinner and to be sure to be home by six.

Which gave her the house to herself all day. She went shopping in the morning, stopping by Barrett's farm for fresh vegetables and then to Trattel's seafood market. Kate's boyfriend, Jack Trattel, was behind the counter and smiled when he saw her.

"We just got some great wild salmon in." It was the only thing she ever bought at the seafood market. Jack had a good memory.

"Perfect, I'll take two pounds, and a couple of lemons, too." She'd forgotten to get the lemons at Bartlett's.

Jack rang her up and handed her the salmon. "Here you go. Enjoy!"

"Thank you. Be sure to tell Kate I said 'hello'."

"I'll do that."

UNLIKE LISA, WHO LOVED TO COOK AND WAS GOOD AT it, Sue did the bare minimum. She had a handful of things she knew how to cook well and rotated through them or more often, ordered takeout. Curt wasn't much of a cook, either, but he liked to grill in the summer and he wasn't picky. He said everything she made was 'outstanding', no matter how ordinary it was. She'd always loved that about him.

Tonight, she was making her 'having company over' dish, lemon salmon. It was the easiest thing in the world to make, and everyone always raved over it. She'd throw some asparagus and potatoes in the oven to roast, and that would be dinner. Lisa said she was bringing dessert, so Sue didn't have to worry about that. And she had plenty of wine on hand. Once she put everything away in the kitchen, she headed upstairs to her office and lost herself in her work for a while.

Sue had started the website a few years back, as an off-shoot of the insurance company's blog. She had taken a course from HubSpot, a company in Cambridge, on content marketing. The idea was to drive traffic to the company website by posting informative articles on the blog on topics people were likely to search online. It worked well, but what surprised Sue was how many requests she'd received from other insurance brokers looking for more information.

So, she'd put up a basic website with more in-depth content on the different topics. Then she developed a few online courses that related to the content, and that's when sales took off. Related podcasts and ebooks followed, and there was no shortage of ideas for new content. Curt didn't understand any of it, that her website was earning them money while they slept as people ordered products and courses. He liked that the money showed up in their account, though, so he didn't complain when she started working from home more as she could still handle most of the day-to-day operations of the agency. Everyone knew she was always available by phone for any questions, though, and she enjoyed helping and trouble-shooting.

At first, Curt had complained that she wasn't in the office enough. But when the bank deposits from the website kept increasing, he asked less often. And once Brandi started, he stopped asking entirely. Sue did try to make it in for the weekly meetings, though, and she enjoyed seeing everyone and hearing how their week went. She usually had a good idea anyway, since she always had several calls with questions from different people throughout the week, and it was all Curt ever talked about—especially how well Brandi was doing.

She was glad that Brandi had turned out to be such a good hire. She hadn't been an inexpensive one. They found most of their people through word of mouth, but when they needed to hire again and that well was dry, they'd worked with a headhunter that specialized in the insurance industry and he found Brandi. The fee was not insignificant, but Brandi quickly paid for herself by bringing in some good new accounts.

Sue thought about what Lisa and Paige had said about Brandi and understood how it may have looked. Brandi was naturally outgoing, and very physical with people. She was an enthusiastic hugger and often touched people's arms when she talked to them. But if you didn't know that about her, she could see how maybe it could raise eyebrows. Especially if a married man like Curt appeared to be hanging on her every word. Knowing Curt, she was pretty sure that he just liked the attention. Curt flirted with women of all ages, but it was harmless.

She turned her attention back to her work and at about four thirty, she stopped for the day and jumped in the shower. Once she was all changed and her hair was dry, she made her way downstairs and got busy in the kitchen, putting the potatoes and asparagus in the oven to roast. She decided to make a big salad with the leafy greens and veggies she'd found earlier.

The very last step was to put the salmon on, but she wasn't even going to do that until Lisa and Rhett arrived. She got everything ready, though—put the fish in the large saute pan and sliced the lemon and butter that she'd add to the pan. It wouldn't take long to cook, and they could snack on cheese, crackers and wine in the meantime.

But by twenty past five, Curt wasn't home yet and Sue started feeling annoyed. She texted him.

'*Where are you?*'

And he immediately replied back, '*on my way*'.

He flew through the door fifteen minutes later and looked a mess. His tie was undone, his sleeves were rolled up, and his hair was all disheveled.

"What on earth have you been up to?"

"I was at Brandi's and she had a plumbing issue. I tried to help, but I think I just made things worse."

"What were you doing at Brandi's?" Sue thought he'd been at the office.

"She had the committee meeting at her place. She wanted to show us her place and just had a new dining room table delivered." He wasn't looking at her, and Sue knew he wasn't telling her everything.

"Who went?"

"What do you mean?"

"Who went to Brandi's? Was it the whole committee?"

"No, not the whole committee." He shifted and reached in the refrigerator for a bottled water. He was evading her question and it was starting to seriously annoy her.

"Who else went besides you and Brandi?" she asked slowly.

There was a long silence. "No one. It was just us."

"Okay. Why didn't the others go?"

"Well, everything was covered in the last meeting, except for the project we're working on. We needed to go over the catering and target list of people to invite."

Sue raised her eyebrows. "The others didn't need to be involved with that?"

"They were initially. This was just a fine-tuning and adjusting what we'd already decided on. I think Brandi was just excited to show off her new place. It is very nice."

"Except for the plumbing issue."

"Well, yeah. It was a good thing I was there, actually, as she didn't know how to turn off the water after the toilet overflowed. I found the shutoff valve and tried to fix it, but it was beyond me, so she called a plumber. And then I realized the time and raced out of there."

"Right. Well, you'd better jump in the shower, and get cleaned up."

CURT CAME BACK DOWNSTAIRS TWENTY MINUTES LATER, dressed in the navy v-neck sweater she'd given him for Christmas with a white t-shirt underneath, his good jeans, and with only slightly damp hair. He was all smiles.

"So, what are we having?"

"What do you think?" As if she ever made anything else.

"Oh, right. Your salmon is great." He fished a wine opener out of a drawer and opened a cupboard to get a wine glass. "Are you ready for a glass?"

Yes, she was most definitely ready. "Sure. Open the pinot noir, that should go well with the fish."

Curt looked through their wine rack until he found the one he was looking for, opened the bottle and poured for both of them. Sue reached for one of the glasses and took a sip. It was a good wine, smooth and fruity and not too light like some pinot noirs tended to be.

Two minutes later there was a knock on the door. It was six sharp and Lisa and Rhett were right on time. She welcomed them in and poured a glass of wine for Lisa and an IPA beer for Rhett. Sue set out a dish with a circle of goat cheese in the middle, smothered with olive oil and fresh herbs.

"Oh, that looks good. Did you make it?" Lisa asked.

Sue laughed at the thought. "No, it came this way at the market." She opened a box of crackers and added them to the plate. Lisa spread a little on a cracker and took a taste.

"That's delicious. Rhett, try one of these." She made him a cracker and he gave it a thumbs up and went back for another.

"Oh, tell me how you do your salmon. I keep meaning to try it myself."

Sue squeezed a lemon over the salmon and added half a stick of butter to the pan, turned the heat on low and covered it.

"That's it. Just lemon, butter and salmon. Cook on low for about twenty minutes and flip it halfway. Even I can't screw it up." She smiled and reached for a cracker to try the cheese.

A half hour later, they sat down to dinner. The salmon, as usual, was perfect. They all chatted easily as they ate.

"Sue tells me you guys are really busy," Lisa commented to Curt. He lit up at the question.

"We are. Everyone is doing a great job. Brandi has been especially impressive. She keeps landing new business for us. I've never seen anything like it."

"She really has done a great job," Sue agreed as she reached for more asparagus.

"And wait until you see what she has planned for A Nantucket Affair. It's going to be the best year yet."

"She's on the committee with Curt," Sue explained.

"Oh, right. That's coming up in a few months," Lisa said.

"It will be here before we know it. We still have a lot to do, but Brandi is so organized that it's all going really smoothly."

"She really sounds like something," Rhett said.

"Oh, she is. We're lucky to have her," Curt gushed. Sue felt a rush of annoyance. Enough already about Brandi.

"So, on a different note, guess what I splurged on this week? It should be arriving in a few days." Curt looked around the table, excited to share his news. Sue hadn't a clue what he was talking about.

"What did you get?" She asked.

"Well, you know how I've been talking about getting a new car?" Curt had a perfectly good Honda CRX—a practical, small SUV. It was close to ten years old, but it didn't have too many miles on it and ran perfectly.

"No, I don't remember you mentioning wanting a new car, actually."

"Maybe I mentioned to someone in the office, then." Brandi, no doubt. "Anyway, I got a sweet deal and a candy apple red Mercedes convertible will soon be mine."

Sue almost dropped her fork. Curt had never been into cars, especially not showy ones.

Rhett whistled. "That sounds like a beauty." Sue knew that Rhett appreciated a nice car. He had a vintage Jaguar that he'd brought to the island for Daffodil Day, when he'd first arrived on the island. But a Mercedes! What was Curt thinking?

"That sounds expensive," she said cautiously.

"Well, it's not new, of course. If it was, that would be insanely expensive. This one is five years old and well maintained. An older couple owned it. It's really a creampuff."

"Whatever made you decide on that car? I thought you loved your Honda?"

"Oh, I do. It's a great car. This is just for fun. And I figure it will look good for the agency."

Sue raised an eyebrow. "How do you figure that?"

"Well, if I'm driving around in that car, I'll look successful. The agency will look successful, I mean and people are attracted to that. New customers, that is."

Sue stared at him, dumbfounded. Her husband had lost his mind.

"I'm not sure that's true. Realtors, maybe, as they are driving clients around. We don't really go anywhere," she said.

"It will look nice parked right out front," he insisted.

Lisa caught her eye and shook her head slightly. The corners of her mouth were turned up, and Sue guessed she was trying not to laugh. Sue changed the subject and they chatted about the kids and other things.

The brownies that Lisa brought were too good. Sue was full, but couldn't resist sharing one with Lisa. The guys didn't hesitate, and each had a full one. By the time they said their goodbyes and Lisa and Rhett left, Sue was tired and ready to fall into bed. But first, she had a few things to say to Curt.

As soon as they were alone, she turned to him.

"What is going on with you? Are you having a mid-life crisis?"

He looked surprised by the question.

"What? Because of the car?"

"That. And your obsession with Brandi. People have noticed, Curt. You're spending a lot of time together and you're obviously fond of each other. She's a pretty girl and a much younger one. Is there anything you're not telling me?" She didn't think there was, but his behavior was frustrating.

He looked offended by the question. "Of course not. Brandi is young enough to be our daughter." She was, in fact, the same age as Stephanie.

"That doesn't matter to a lot of people," she said.

"I'm sorry. I never thought about how it might look. It's totally innocent, but you know that. I will admit, though, that I like the attention. Brandi is good for my ego."

For a moment, Sue felt hurt. "I'm not good for your ego?"

He looked at her quite seriously. "Honestly, lately you haven't wanted to be around me much. You never want to come out with us. Sometimes it seems like I'm bothering you, so yeah, I've enjoyed flirting with Brandi a little. It's harmless. It's just how I am, you know that."

She sighed. "I know. It's just when other people mention it to me that it's embarrassing. If anyone had seen you going to her house today—well, that's how rumors get started."

"I suppose you're right about that. She was just so excited to show me her place. She said I'm the first person that she's had over." That made Sue wonder about Brandi's intentions. Was she as innocent as Curt seemed to think?

"She needs to make some more friends," Sue said dryly.

"So, are we okay? What do you think about the car?"

"I think it would have been nice if you'd mentioned it to me before you bought it. Why didn't you?" He didn't need to ask her permission, and they had the money for the car. She was just surprised that he didn't think to ask her opinion before he made the decision to buy.

A sheepish look crossed his face. "I didn't want you to try to talk me out of it. You know you would have. It's completely frivolous, and you're right, my car is fine. It's just that I wanted to splurge. I test drove it last weekend and it's so fun to drive." Sue didn't doubt that.

"Wait, did you say you test drove it last weekend? You went off-island?"

She knew that he definitely hadn't mentioned that. Unless she was losing her mind.

"It was a spur-of-the-moment thing. You weren't home and I just went. I was home by dinner. I just had to go check it out. And I'm glad I did."

"Well, I'm glad you got it, then, if it made you that

happy." He looked like a little kid, he was so excited about the new car.

"So, you wouldn't be feeling romantic by any chance, would you? We could go upstairs and celebrate the new car." He was serious. But there was no way. Sue couldn't shift gears that quickly. She was still annoyed that he hadn't told her about the car, and she felt uneasy about the whole Brandi situation. She believed Curt, that there was nothing there. But he was still drawn to Brandi. She gave him something that Sue didn't right now. He was basking in her attention. It felt like the two of them just weren't on the same page lately.

"Not tonight. I'm too tired."

Disappointment flashed across Curt's face, but he just nodded. "All right. I'm going to head up to bed then."

"I'm right behind you. I'm going to stop in the office for a minute and just check some emails first."

CHAPTER 19

When Beth arrived home the next day, Chase was out but he'd left her a note and a box of her favorite dark chocolate caramels with sea salt. She smiled. Some guys did flowers, but Chase knew she much preferred sweets. His note was short and sweet.

"I'm sorry I was a jerk. Forgive me?" As if there was any doubt. She opened the box and popped a chocolate in her mouth. They were from Sweet Inspirations, her favorite place for chocolates on Nantucket.

While she waited for Chase to come home, Beth did her laundry for the week and cleaned up a bit. Unlike Angela, Beth hated cleaning, and Chase wasn't too fond of it, either. They both pitched in and it really wasn't too bad as their place was small. Someday, when they could justify the expense and were living elsewhere, they'd hire Angela's company.

Beth finished the laundry and cleaning and had just flopped down on the sofa to watch a little TV when Chase walked in. He saw her and grinned, as she was holding the box of chocolates and had just put one in her mouth. He sat down next to her.

"Does this mean I'm forgiven?" He glanced at the chocolates.

Beth laughed. "Does what mean you're forgiven? I'm just sitting here eating chocolate. They're very good. Would you like one?" She held the box out and he grabbed one.

"I really am sorry. I've just been a grouch. It was a stressful week and we just have to be so careful now with expenses on the flip house."

"I know. It's been stressing me out, too, but I'm just trying to stay positive. And of course you're forgiven." She leaned toward him and his lips met hers for a quick kiss.

"Good, because I hated that we fought. You're the most important person in my life."

"It was our first real disagreement. I'm sure it won't be our last. I hated it, too. You're the last person I want to fight with."

"So, if you're interested, I thought maybe we'd grab a bite to eat somewhere? Are you in the mood for anything in particular?"

Beth thought about it for a moment. "How about the Thai place? We haven't been there in a while and it's inexpensive."

"Sounds good to me."

LATER, OVER DINNER, CHASE TURNED THE DISCUSSION back to the flip house.

"I think if all goes well, we should be finished in just about two weeks. Lauren called yesterday and said she's already told some of her buyers that she has a great property coming soon. She suggested an open house again, no showings until that day. Maybe we can collect multiple offers."

"Wouldn't that be nice?" With all the unexpected expenses, Beth was hoping to just break even. Anything more would be a very welcome bonus. And multiple offers would give them a better chance for a good profit.

"A few more flip houses, and then we might want to start thinking about taking some of that money for a down payment on our own dream house."

That was the first time Chase floated the idea of them building a house together, and Beth saw he was watching her closely to see her reaction. Her heart filled. They hadn't actually talked about marriage yet but since they were living together, she'd assumed that eventually they'd get there.

"I love that idea. Assuming there's some profit left on this one."

"There will be. I'm feeling better about it now. It's a great house."

They'd just ordered dessert and when the waiter brought the cheesecake with cherries to the table for them to split, Chase surprised her by standing up, and then getting down on one knee. The air in the small restaurant seemed to still and Beth was vaguely aware of other tables turning their way.

Chase held up a small black velvet box.

"Beth, when I asked you to move in, I knew that this day would come because there was no doubt then or now that you're the person I want to spend forever with. And even if we fight now and then, I want us to always come home together and to make up. The making up could be fun, actually." He smiled and opened the box. An absolutely gorgeous princess cut diamond was surrounded by smaller ones on a pretty gold setting.

"What do you think? Want to get married —to me?"

Beth felt a rush of emotion overwhelm her and couldn't speak for a moment. She could see that her hesitation was unexpected and there was a hint of nervousness in his eyes. And then the words came out in a rush.

"Of course. I'd love to."

Chase stood and slipped the ring on her finger. It dazzled, even though the restaurant lighting was soft.

She couldn't stop staring at the ring. He'd surprised her totally. She certainly hadn't expected a proposal today.

He kissed her, then sat back down and admired the ring on her finger.

"It looks good on you."

"It does. You did well." She grinned. "Your mother is going to be thrilled."

"That she is."

CHAPTER 20

On Sunday, as usual, Sue went to visit her mother at Dover Falls. When she walked in the door, her mother was dressed in her Sunday best, and was sitting at a round table playing cards with three other residents. She smiled when she saw Sue, then looked around the table.

"Ladies, looks like I won't be taking any more of your money today. Time to go visit with my daughter." The women all said hello to Sue as her mother gathered up her pile of dollar bills.

They went into the dining room and found a sunny table by a window. Over a delicious lunch of chicken pot pie and mashed potatoes, her mother filled her in on all the goings on since she'd last seen her.

"So, Ethel and Harry just got engaged! At their age, can you imagine? Ethel's never been married, though, so I guess why not, right? Harry's a nice enough guy. Donna wasn't happy about that, though. Not at all. She set her cap on Harry months ago, but he never took any notice of her."

"That's great. Good for Ethel." Sue thought it sounded romantic to finally find love in her eighties and to get married.

"Well, enough about me. Let's talk about you. Where is that husband of yours?"

"He's off-island picking up a new car. They called this morning and told him it was ready, so he was going to head over and pick it up."

"I didn't realize he needed a new car. Did he get another Honda?"

Sue smiled. "Not exactly. He still has the Honda. He got a bright red Mercedes convertible."

Her mother laughed. "What on earth does he need that for?"

"He doesn't. He just wanted it. He says it will make him look successful and the agency, too."

"Oh, that's just silly. He wants to be seen driving it all over the island. He's clearly going through a mid-life crisis."

"That crossed my mind, too."

"What about that young blonde girl in the office, Barbi something? Is he still spending too much time with her?"

"It's Brandi, and they are on a committee together.

We talked about it, actually. I told him people have commented and he said that's ridiculous, that there's nothing to comment on. I'm really not worried about Curt."

"No, I don't suppose you should be. He's not the type, I don't think. Besides you have a wonderful, happy marriage so nothing to worry about."

Sue was quiet and her mother raised her eyebrow. "Everything is fine, right?"

"Yes, it's fine. I suppose." She sighed. "Though we don't spend as much time together as we used to. I work from home now and Curt's so busy with work at the office and so involved in so many social things, like the Nantucket Affair event. They keep asking him to chair it."

"And Brandi's on that committee? And works with him? So, she's seeing him almost as much as you are?"

"Well, in a different way, but yes, I suppose so."

"So, she's giving him the attention he's not getting from you? When was the last time you two had a date night?"

Sue laughed. "We go out with friends all the time. You know I'm not much for cooking."

"That's not what I mean. When was the last time you went out for a romantic evening? Where you both got dressed up and had a lovely dinner and conversation and maybe even some dancing?"

"Gosh, I don't remember the last time we did that.

Maybe a year or so ago when we spent the weekend in Boston and went to the theater."

"Maybe it's time to see a show," her mother suggested.

"I'll think about it. The next month or so is really busy."

Her mother sipped her tea and glanced out the window before turning back to Sue with a serious look.

"A good marriage takes work to keep it good. To keep the romance going. If you don't make the effort and spend too much time apart, it will just get harder to find your way back. Trust me on that."

"What are you talking about? You and Daddy had one of the best relationships I've ever seen." Sue's father had been gone for just over five years now, and as far as she knew her parents had always been madly in love.

"Your father was the love of my life but we went through a rough period, when you and your brother were in middle school. You kids got most of my attention then and work got most of his. We stopped going out for date nights because we were both so busy and tired." She was quiet, and her eyes grew dark for a moment before she smiled and said, "But fortunately, we realized we needed to make time for each other. We started the date nights again and the magic came back. It never left after that."

Sue guessed there was more to the story than her mother was willing to share, but that was okay. She got the point. They moved on to other topics until after a few lively hours of conversation, her mother started to look tired. When she couldn't fight back a yawn, Sue stood and stretched.

"I should probably head home. A pile of laundry is calling my name."

"A nap might be calling mine." She stood too and walked Sue to the door.

"Next time Curt comes with you, tell him he has to drive that fancy new car and take me for a spin!"

"I'll tell him. He'd love that."

It was still light out when Sue got home and she was looking forward to seeing Curt's new car. She expected him back before it got dark, so when six o'clock rolled around and there was no sign of Curt, she called his cell. But he didn't pick up and it went to voicemail. She didn't leave a message. She figured he'd see the missed call and call her back. That's what they usually did for each other, unless it was urgent and a message was needed.

At six-thirty, he finally called and she was torn between being worried and annoyed.

"Where are you? I thought you'd be home by now. Did you get the car?"

"I did and it's a beauty. Wait til you see it. I'm just leaving the Club Car now. I met up with Tom and

John for a drink. I'll be home soon. Sorry I missed your call. My phone was dead and I had it on Tom's charger."

"Have you eaten yet? I was thinking we could go grab dinner, maybe."

"Shoot, I wish I'd known you wanted to go out. I just had a burger."

"Oh. I guess I'll heat up a frozen pizza or something."

"Okay, see you in ten."

In exactly ten minutes, Sue heard the sound of a car pulling in the driveway. Curt was home. But it was too dark out to see the new car well. She walked outside to take a look, anyway.

"So, what do you think?"

"What I can see of it looks nice. I'll get a better look tomorrow."

Curt followed her inside. She'd just taken her pizza out of the microwave right before he got home and settled back in her seat at the island to continue eating. Curt leaned against the counter while she ate.

"How was your mom?"

"She's good. I told her about the car. She said she wants a ride."

He liked that. "Excellent. I'll drive next time we go see her and take her for a spin."

"How was the Club Car? Anyone else there we know?"

"Yeah, Paige and Peter were there, actually. Paige

gave the car a thumbs up. And Brandi was there with a friend, sitting at the bar."

Of course she was. Brandi was always out.

"I suppose she loved the car, too?"

He nodded. "Everyone did. It's a great car."

"How are Tom and John?" They were Curt's best friends. Sue was friends with Tom's wife, Linda. John was very much single. He'd been divorced for just over five years and wasn't in any hurry to get serious with anyone again. But he loved to date.

"They're good. Tom and Linda just booked a cruise to Bermuda. And John is John. Tom and I actually left at the same time, but John stayed to have another drink with Brandi and her friend. I can't imagine Brandi would be interested in someone his age, but maybe her friend is."

Sue just smiled. For a relatively smart man, Curt could be dumb sometimes.

"John is a handsome man, and well off. Plenty of women like that and don't mind dating an older man."

"Maybe." He still looked doubtful.

"So, remember our trip to Boston last year? I was thinking it might be fun to do something like that again soon. What do you think?"

"Sure, though might be good to wait a month or so, after A Nantucket Affair. We still have a lot of work to do to get ready."

"I'll keep an eye on what's coming and maybe we'll book something after that."

Curt yawned. "Sounds good. I'm going to go watch some golf on TV for a while."

He headed off to the living room while she finished her pizza, then went upstairs to change into her pajamas and read in bed for a while. She thought a lot about what her mother had said earlier, and as she drifted off to sleep, an idea came to her.

CHAPTER 21

Tyler adjusted fairly quickly to the environment at Murphy House. It was similar to the first rehab he went to, so he knew what to expect. The first few days were the hardest, because the physical craving for alcohol was fierce. But he was kept busy with lots of different counseling sessions, some were one-on-one and others were group sessions. And they got a lot of physical exercise, which helped burn off frustrations.

The ages ranged from eighteen to mid-fifties and several of the guys, like Tyler, had been through the rehab process before. As they went around the room sharing their stories in group sessions, one thing that stood out was the shame they all felt from relapsing and disappointing the people they cared for. Some of them had triggers like Tyler—a loved one dying unexpectedly, a divorce, or a job loss. But others couldn't pinpoint any trigger in particular beyond a strong desire for a drink that they tried to resist until it was impossible and they gave in.

One of the guys, Ben, was a successful bond trader and spoke about how his life really couldn't be better and he still screwed up.

"I just got engaged a month ago, to a great girl from a good family. Her dad actually owns the financial services firm that I work for. And work is going great. I'm one of their top traders. But expectations are high and there's a lot of pressure. I think I worry sometimes that I don't deserve to be so successful and that it could all disappear at any moment. Amy could realize I'm not the guy she wants to spend the rest of her life with. It just got to the point where the little voice calling for a drink got louder every day."

Tyler could relate to that, too. He thought he'd been handling his mother's death okay and he had Kristen, who was amazing. He should have been able to resist, and it scared the hell out of him that he'd fallen. He wouldn't blame her if she bailed like his wife did. Who would want to sign up for dealing with this? The fear of that happening again had only made him crave another drink even more. The alcohol numbed everything and let him put his head in the sand and just not deal.

But he was feeling stronger after two weeks at Murphy House. Kristen was coming this Saturday for a visit, and he was both nervous and anxious to see her at the same time. He knew it was asking a lot of her to stick with him. It was helping to talk everything through, and to be in an environment where alcohol wasn't an option. And he wouldn't be going home until his counselors and he both felt that he was ready and able to resist temptation.

He'd done it before, and he knew he could do it again. As long as he just didn't take the first drink again, he'd be fine. He envied Kristen and all his other friends who could have one drink and call it a day. His off button was missing, so the only option was to never turn it on.

ANDREW PICKED KRISTEN UP AND THEY DROVE ONTO the slow boat, which was the only option for taking a vehicle off Nantucket. Once they landed in Hyannis, they drove another forty minutes or so to Falmouth. Kristen didn't really know what to expect, maybe more of a hospital setting. But when they arrived, it was actually a large, Victorian house with lots of land around it that was nicely landscaped.

They met Tyler in a sitting area full of sofas and comfy chairs. He looked good. His hair was getting a little long, but she'd always liked it best right before he got it cut, when the waves touched his collar bone. He was freshly shaved and his face had more color than it usually did.

"You look good," Andrew said immediately. "Have you been outside much?"

"Yeah, I've been running with a few of the guys and playing some pickup basketball in the afternoons when the weather is good." That explained his rosy cheeks. Normally, Tyler was holed up inside and didn't have the best eating habits, especially when on a writing—or a drinking—binge.

"You guys look great, too. Is that a new sweater?" Tyler glanced at the periwinkle blue soft sweater Kristen had actually bought just a few days before.

"Yeah, it is new. I'm glad you like it."

They chatted about easy stuff, mostly. Tyler told them all about the place and what his days were like. Kristen hadn't realized it was so structured and with so many kinds of counseling.

"It sounds like you're too busy to get much writing done."

He smiled. "Oddly enough, I'm more productive this past week than I was before I came here. I've had to fit the writing in, so I've been getting up earlier and getting the words in first thing. They seem to come easier when I'm not fully awake, and then I'm mostly done for the day."

"Oh, that sounds good then." She paused and then asked the question she and Andrew really wanted to know. "How are you feeling? Will you be ready to come home in two weeks, do you think?"

He nodded. "I will be. This has been really good for

me. Just talking to the counselors and the other guys, too. Everyone is going through different stuff, but it's helpful to just talk it out. I have lots of good reasons to stay sober, and I don't want to mess that up again.

"I'm sorry that I drank around you. I'll be more careful from now on."

But Tyler grabbed her hand and looked her in the eye.

"I don't want you to do that. You having a glass of wine has nothing to do with me being here. I'm totally okay around other people that are drinking. It's my issue, not theirs. The only reason I didn't want to go to that dinner party was because I was already drinking—when I'm sober, it's not a problem. I can have a non-alcoholic beer or just soda water."

"Okay. Well, we won't worry about that then." But Kristen was going to cut back when she was around Tyler, at least until she was really sure that he was fine and not likely to relapse again."

A little while later, Andrew excused himself to use the rest room. Kristen guessed he wanted to give the two of them a little privacy.

"I miss you," Kristen said simply. "I'm glad that it's going well here, though."

"You have no idea how much I miss you. I worried that I might have lost you. That this was all too much." He looked away for a moment, then added, "I wouldn't blame you if it was. It's a lot." By the frown lines on his forehead, Kristen sensed that he'd been worrying about this a lot and she tried to reassure him.

"I'm not going anywhere. We can get through this. You getting better is the most important thing. And you have a good support system, between your brother, me, my whole family and your sponsor." Scotty sounded like a good guy. Kristen hadn't met him yet, but Tyler obviously thought highly of him.

"Scotty's the best. I know I'm lucky to have all of you on my side. It really is going well. I feel better and stronger each day. I'm working through some stuff in the counseling sessions. It's all helping. Hopefully, you'll never have to come here again."

Kristen grinned. "Well, we are bringing you home in two weeks, so I will be back then."

He laughed. "That's different."

"We'll get through this," Kristen said again, to emphasize that she wasn't going anywhere.

"Thank you." Tyler looked up as Andrew returned and sat down again. "Thanks to both of you for coming, and for just being there. It means a lot. It really does."

They chatted a little while longer and then it was time to leave to catch the ferry back home. Andrew hugged Tyler goodbye and then Kristen wrapped her arms around him and squeezed him tight. "I'm proud of you for coming here and doing the work to get better," she said softly. "And I can't wait to see you in two weeks and bring you home."

He kissed her softly, a quick peck that spoke volumes. "Thank you, for everything."

Once Kristen and Andrew were back in his car and heading toward the boat, Kristen asked what was on her mind.

"How do you think he's doing? Is this what it was like the first time he went in?"

"No. Night and day different, really. He was way worse that first time. He was in a really bad place and hadn't really accepted that he even had a problem with drinking. He resisted treatment then, but now he seems to have embraced it. I thought he seemed great and I think it will be different this time. I mean, you never do know, but he seems strong this time. And he has more reasons to stick to it."

"That's reassuring. I hope you're right."

CHAPTER 22

When Curt came into the kitchen Monday morning, he did a double-take when he saw Sue, sitting at the island, sipping coffee and instead of wearing her usual sweats, she was fully dressed in her favorite gray pants and pink cashmere sweater.

"You look nice today. Do you have an appointment somewhere?"

He poured himself a cup and joined her.

"Thanks. No appointment. I actually thought I might come into the office today for a change."

Curt set his cup down in surprise. "Really? On a Monday? Any particular reason?"

"It's something I've been thinking about recently. I like working from home, but it feels a little too separate, not as connected with you and the company as maybe I should be. I thought I might come in a few days a week and see how it goes."

Curt smiled. "Well, I'm all for it. I gave up asking you to come in more, but that would be great. Your office hasn't been touched, as you know. So, you can jump right in. We can ride in together if you like. I'm taking Betty on her first official outing."

Sue almost spit out her coffee. "You named your car Betty?"

"Yep. Seemed to fit her. So, what do you say? I'm ready to go when you are."

"I'll walk out with you, but I'm going to take my own car. I'm thinking I might work the morning in the office and at home in the afternoon."

Sue finished her coffee, then followed Curt outside and admired Betty as he got in and put her top down. She had to admit, the Mercedes convertible was a beautiful car and it was a lovely day to be driving it. The sun was shining, the air was warm and there was no wind.

She followed him in her white Volkswagen Jetta and smiled when she saw where he parked—the closest spot to the door, so everyone would see the car as they walked in.

They were the first ones in the office. Curt always liked to get in early and both of them felt that as owners, it set a good example for the rest. Sue settled into her office, made a fresh cup of coffee and was just going through some emails when Brandi walked through the door followed a moment later by everyone else. At first no one noticed that Sue was in her office, until Mary, the secretary/receptionist, walked by and did a double-take. She back stepped and stuck her head in the office.

"Well, this is a nice surprise! I've missed seeing you here."

"Thanks, Mary. I thought I might spend a few mornings a week in the office. I miss it."

"Well, that's good news for all of us. If you need anything, let me know."

Brandi stopped by a moment later. "I'm so sorry, I didn't even notice you were in today. Curt didn't mention that we'd be seeing you."

"He just found out this morning. I decided over the weekend that I want to spend more time here. I can help better when I'm more available."

"Are you going to be here every day now?" Brandi looked surprised.

"I'm not exactly sure yet. I'm going to take it day by day."

"Well, welcome back then! I have a call in a few minutes, so, I have to run. Have a good day." Sue watched her walk back to her desk. She had to admit, the dress she was wearing was gorgeous. It was a pretty peach, and it fit her slim curves perfectly and fell just above her knee. Her strappy high heels showed off her toned calves. Brandi looked like she worked out often, was careful what she ate and it paid off. Everything looked good on her.

Sue had thought her own outfit looked nice, but the gray pants had an elastic waist which made them more comfortable than stylish and her pink sweater was pretty but long and loose, to cover her tummy, which was not anywhere near as flat as Brandi's. She tried not to let it bother her though. Twenty years ago when she was Brandi's age, her stomach was flat, too.

The morning flew and Sue felt almost like she'd never left. Since she was in the office, almost everyone had stopped by either to say hello or to ask a quick question and it was a good feeling to be able to help. Sue knew just about all the client accounts and knew the insurance industry inside and out. Curt even popped in mid-morning to ask about a client that they'd had forever.

"Tricia Thompson wants to know if we'll give her a referral bonus for sending her two sisters to us. I know we talked about putting a referral program into place, but we haven't gotten there yet. What are your thoughts?"

Sue considered it for about two seconds. "She's referring us both of her sisters? Absolutely. Let's do two hundred dollars off her homeowner's policy, that's a hundred for each sister. Sound good?"

"I like it! Thanks."

At a few minutes to noon, Mary stopped by to ask what kind of pizza she liked.

"You're ordering pizza?" Sue hadn't even thought about lunch yet, but at the mention of pizza her stomach rumbled.

Mary nodded. "Every Monday we bring pizza or some other takeout in for the weekly kickoff meeting in the conference room."

"Oh." That was new. She liked the idea, though.

"I'm easy, I'll eat anything. What do we have so far?"

"A cheese, pepperoni, and a Hawaiian."

"I'm good with any of those."

Forty minutes later, the pizzas were delivered and they all went into the conference room. Sue noticed that Brandi had one slice of Hawaiian pizza. Who could have just one slice of pizza? Sue had three and enjoyed every bite. While they ate, Curt led the discussion on what everyone was working on for the week and what the overall pipeline looked like for the month.

She was impressed by the way Curt led the team. He was enthusiastic, encouraging and helped everyone to challenge themselves by setting higher goals. They also talked about what their biggest challenges were and what they needed help with. Brandi was the first to speak.

"I have a meeting on Friday with John Smithers. He was referred to me and said he's thinking of changing his insurance carrier but is talking to a few different brokers before deciding. Any suggestions on how to position our offering over the others?"

"What's driving his decision? Is it price or a particular kind of coverage?"

Brandi smiled. "Both, of course."

"Okay, why don't you send me an email with the info you know he's looking for. I'll see how flexible we can be and give you some ideas on how to pitch it."

"Great, thank you."

After the lunch meeting, Sue wrapped up a few emails and then got ready to head out to work from home the rest of the afternoon on the website. She went to say goodbye to Curt and saw that Brandi was leaning against his desk, chatting with him. They both looked up when Sue walked over.

"I'm about to head out. I'll see you at home later. Do you want to pick up some takeout on your way?"

Curt and Brandi exchanged glances. "I'm not sure what time I'm going to be home. We have a meeting right after work tonight at Millie's. I figured I'd grab a bite there. I should be home by around seven. I don't think it's going to take too long."

"Rick called a little while ago and the designs came in for the swag bags. We need to pick one and start putting together a list for silent auction donations," Brandi said.

Sue tried not to feel resentful that the Nantucket Affair event was taking up so much of Curt's time and that Brandi was right there with him. After all, it was a Monday night and if she was being honest with herself, she was looking forward to curling up on the sofa. She could get her own takeout.

"All right. I'll see you at home then." She glanced at Brandi, "And I'll see you tomorrow."

ON SATURDAY, SUE MET UP WITH LISA AND PAIGE FOR A late breakfast at Black-Eyed Susan's off Main Street. They hadn't gone there in ages, and it was nice to relax and catch up over coffee and eggs.

"I can't believe Chase is engaged. Beth really does seem perfect for him. You must be thrilled," Sue said. Lisa had called both of them right after Chase had shared the news.

"Have they set a date yet?" Paige asked.

"Yes, I am thrilled. And no, I don't think they are in any hurry. I'm guessing it may be a year or two. They want to save up and build their house first."

"How is their flip house coming along? They seem to be doing really well with those," Sue said.

"I think it's going okay. Chase has been a little quieter about this one so far. From a few comments they've made, I know they ran into some unexpected expenses. He hasn't said so, but I'm guessing he might be a little worried that this one might not be as profitable as the others."

"When I watch those real estate shows, it looks like such a fun thing to do. But I don't know a thing about construction. I'd probably end up losing my shirt," Paige said.

"Isn't that Brandi, from your office? Isn't that John, Curt's friend? Are they dating?" Lisa was looking out the window and Brandi was standing on the street corner chatting with John.

"I don't think so, but I'm not sure. Curt actually introduced her to a friend when they ran into them recently at the Club Car. Curt thought he was much too old for Brandi, but who knows what Brandi thinks?" A moment later, John took Brandi's arm and they walked off together.

"They looked pretty cozy just now. How is Curt?" Paige asked.

"He's the same as ever. Still so busy between work and A Nantucket Affair."

"That takes a lot of his time, huh?" Lisa sympathized.

"It does. I never used to mind it."

"Well, there wasn't a cute, thirty-something blonde on the committee last year," Paige said dryly.

"I saw my mother on Sunday. She had some good advice. Turned out she and my father went through a rough patch years ago. I had no idea. She said they weren't spending enough time together, and once they made an effort to do that, everything was fine."

"That is good advice. Marriage is work," Lisa agreed.

"That's what she said. I think honestly we're both

so comfortable with each other at this point that we maybe take each other for granted a little too much."

"So, what's your plan?" Paige asked.

"Just to make more of an effort, about everything. I started going back into the office this week. Just mornings, except for Thursday. I was there all day and after the weekly meeting I went out for drinks with everyone."

"Wow, that's a big change," Lisa said.

"I think it's a good one. I was becoming too much of a hermit at home. I wasn't even always making the weekly meeting and I think Curt stopped asking me to do things because I was always saying no."

Paige poured a little more coffee into her mug. "How is it being in the office with Brandi?"

"It's interesting, actually. She's probably the hardest worker in the office, so I have no complaints there. She's not afraid to ask for help either, and we worked together on a project that turned out well."

"Oh, that's good, then," Lisa said.

"I feel kind of frumpy next to her, though. She has the most gorgeous clothes. I might feel a shopping trip coming on, if either of you are up for it? I just haven't bought anything new in ages."

"Well, first of all, you're not frumpy. And of course I'd be up for a shopping trip, maybe next weekend. Paige, are you in?"

"I'm in. Peter and I were going to go away next

weekend, but we had to postpone it because he is short-handed at the store."

"Things are still going well with Peter?" Sue asked. She thought they made a fantastic couple.

"Really well. For the first time for me, it's just easy and we're enjoying each other's company. Took me a long time to learn that relationships don't have to be full of drama. I don't miss that."

"That's how it was with Rhett, too. I just enjoyed his company as a friend first and never really expected more than that. You just never know. He did a sleep study two nights ago and learned that he has sleep apnea."

"Peter has that," Paige said. "Tell Rhett not to freak out about the mask. He'll get used to it, and it will save his life. Sleep apnea is very treatable."

"I'll tell him. He's not too keen about the thought of wearing a mask and hose that will blow air into his face. I think he's embarrassed at the idea of it."

"Tell him not to worry and that it doesn't have to slow anything down in the bedroom. He'll just wait to put the mask on when he's ready to sleep."

Lisa laughed. "Oh, my goodness. Maybe I'll just have him call you and you can tell him that. Or actually, I should just tell him to talk to Peter. That might be a good idea."

"What were his symptoms?" Sue had heard of sleep apnea but wasn't exactly sure what it was.

"He snores and when I got up one night to use the

bathroom, I noticed that he stopped breathing a few times in between snores. He was also saying that he always felt tired and couldn't seem to get a good night's sleep."

"How did they test him for that?"

"He went to a sleep lab in Hyannis for a night. They hooked him up to a bunch of sensors and monitored his sleep. When he had more than fifteen apneas in an hour, they woke him up and fitted him with a CPAP mask and hooked him up to the machine that sends air into the lungs, which keeps the airway open, so there are no interruptions in breathing."

It all sounded somewhat terrifying to Sue. But she was glad that it was treatable and according to Paige, not as bad as it seemed.

"I hope it works well for him," she said.

"I hope so too. We'll find out soon enough. His machine should be arriving sometime next week. I'll fill you in when we go shopping next weekend."

"Perfect. Oh, I meant to ask earlier, how are Kristen and Tyler doing? Is he home yet from his treatment?"

"He comes home next weekend. Kristen and Andrew are picking him up on Saturday. They saw him two weeks ago and were both encouraged by the visit. I hope for both their sakes that he is able to stay sober. Kristen is the one I worry about. That's a lot to deal with."

CHAPTER 23

When the flip house was totally done, Chase and Beth met Lauren there so she could take pictures for the online listing and for flyers to hand out at the open house. Beth felt mostly relief as they walked around the house with Lauren. It had turned out beautifully. Hopefully, the open house would attract multiple offers and they'd be able to make some profit.

"I love the backsplash you did in the kitchen," Lauren said.

Chase looked her way and smiled. "That was all Beth. I wanted to cheap out and use a different one, but she insisted."

"Good, that was smart. Gives it a rich look. Buyers, especially on Nantucket, love that. And Chase, nice job opening up this room. Everyone wants open-concept and this makes it look so much bigger."

Once Lauren got all the pictures she needed, they left and she agreed to keep them posted.

"I'll do the open house next Saturday and will hopefully call Sunday with an offer—or two. Cross your fingers."

Chase helped Lauren pound a for sale sign in the front yard, before she climbed into her white BMW and drove off. Chase wrapped his arms around Beth's waist from behind, and they both stared back at the house for a moment.

"It's out of our hands now. Let's hope Lauren can work her usual magic," Beth said.

"It's too soon to celebrate, but how about going for a beer, anyway? We can toast to being done and having the house come out awesome."

"Lead the way."

THE FOLLOWING SUNDAY, CHASE AND BETH WERE lounging on their sofa, being lazy. They were also anxious to hear from Lauren. She'd called the day before and said there had been a good turnout for the open house. Several people seemed seriously interested and that they'd get back to her. None had said the word offer, though, which made both of them nervous.

"It's perfectly normal if no offers come right away. Houses don't always sell from open houses," Beth said. They knew that was true. Lauren was just so good, though, and had brought them offers twice before right after open houses, so their expectations and hopes were high.

When seven o'clock rolled around and they still hadn't heard anything further from Lauren, Beth sighed. "I guess it wasn't very realistic to expect an offer that fast. We've been spoiled."

"I'm not worried. It will sell. It just might not be as fast as we'd hoped."

At eight thirty, Chase's cell phone rang, and it was Lauren. He answered and put it on speakerphone so Beth could hear.

"So, I'm sorry to call so late, but I have good news. Really good news. I'm late calling because," she paused dramatically, "I was waiting for a second offer! We have two good offers!" She went on to explain the details of the two offers. They were twenty thousand dollars apart, but the lower offer was a cash offer. They wouldn't have to wait for the buyer to secure financing.

"What else can you tell us about the buyers?" Beth asked.

"Well, the cash offer is from an established couple here on the island and I think they want to buy it for one of their kids. The other offer is a young couple with a baby and it would be their first home. He works remotely for a big software company, and she works part time at Pacific National Bank on Main Street.

"Well, that's great news. Thank you. Beth and I will discuss and give you a call back."

He ended the call and turned to Beth. "So, what do

you think? Kind of a no-brainer, right? Should I call Lauren back and say we're taking the higher offer?" Beth wasn't surprised that he immediately wanted to go with that offer. It was quite a bit more money.

"Well, maybe. What if we asked her to counter-offer the cash people by twenty thousand and let them know we have another offer, but if they can do that we'll take it?"

"That's not a bad idea at all. I like it. Best of both worlds." Chase called Lauren back and she agreed to present the counteroffer to the cash buyers.

They didn't hear anything further until the next day at lunchtime. Chase and Beth were both in the office when Lauren called.

"Bad news, I'm afraid. They rejected your counteroffer."

"Shoot. Did they come up at all?" Chase asked.

"No, they said they are comfortable with the original offer and if it doesn't work out, they saw another house they might go with. Discuss and call me back!"

"So, we go with the higher offer, right? We could really use that twenty thousand."

Beth hesitated. She hated to say no to a cash offer as she'd seen so many real estate deals fall apart at the last minute. But still, twenty thousand was too much money to say no to.

"Go ahead and call her back."

CHAPTER 24

"I really can't stand this thing." Rhett scowled at the CPAP mask he was about to put on. It was his third night wearing it and so far, neither he or Lisa had slept much. He just wasn't used to it and either had it on too tight or too loose, and ended up pulling it off in the middle of the night. Every time he struggled with it or got up, it woke Lisa, too. She was sleeping more lightly because she was worried about him getting sleep. Eventually, he'd get it back on and they'd both fall asleep again.

Over breakfast Saturday morning before Lisa was heading off-island to go shopping, Rhett was in a rare grumpy mood.

"I don't think I'm ever going to get used to that thing. I might just take a break from it for a few days."

Lisa took a sip of her coffee and considered her words. "You could do that. But do you remember what the doctor said? That if it stays untreated, there is the possibility of sudden cardiac arrest. You could go to sleep and never wake up. If you don't mind that, then by all means take a break. I would miss you, though, if anything happened. Just saying."

Rhett sighed. "I hate when you make perfect sense and I'm an idiot. Fine, I'll wear the stupid thing."

"Did you give Peter a call like I suggested? He's worn one for years and might set your mind at ease."

"No, I totally forgot. I will call him." He topped off his coffee and sat back down. "How are bookings this week? Still steady?"

Lisa pulled out her smartphone and searched for the Airbnb booking site.

"It has been steady. I haven't looked yet this morning to see if any new reservations came in." The site loaded, and she was happy to see that the one vacant room she had left for the next day was just filled. She smiled and scrolled down to look at the newest reviews. There were three new ones. Two were five-star reviews, but best of all one of them was the one-star from the Laceys that was changed to a five.

"Looks like maybe my strategy worked," Lisa said.

"What strategy is that?"

"Well, remember that one-star review from the Laceys? Turns out the wife is a friend of Lillian's that owns the Red Rose Bed and Breakfast. He said he was going to talk to his wife and have her change that review, but until today it was unchanged. But a few days ago, I referred some business to Lillian."

"Why on earth would you do that?"

"Well, to service my customer, for one thing. The Hardys wanted to extend their stay on Nantucket, but their room was already booked after their initial end date. They wanted something similar, so I called Lillian to see if she had a room and she was surprised and appreciative of the referral. I told her I'd be happy to continue sending people her way if we were full."

"Oh, that was smart."

"I did casually drop mention of the review into the conversation too and how the husband was horrified but the wife had yet to change the review, which was such a disappointment. I didn't mention that I knew they knew her. But it's interesting how it immediately came down."

"Good. All is as it should be, then. All right, while you go shopping, maybe I'll go try to take a nap and see if I can get that mask to cooperate."

CHAPTER 25

K ndash risten called Andrew and told him that she was fine going by herself to pick up Tyler. She knew he would have to find someone to watch the gallery, and she thought it might be nice for them to have some time alone.

She drove onto the Steamship Authority and settled in to read for a few hours until they reached Hyannis. It was hard for her to concentrate on the story, though, as her mind was whirling, going from excitement to see Tyler to worry about him staying sober. She wanted to support and help him as best as she could, but she wasn't sure what that meant, what she could do. But she figured that going to the Al-Anon meetings would help her learn, and that she'd get support there for herself, too.

Tyler was waiting downstairs when she arrived. He didn't have much with him, just a giant duffle bag and his laptop. He smiled when he saw her, and her heart did a flip. He looked like the Tyler she'd first met, healthy and handsome. He'd had his hair cut just a little, and it looked good. And he was wearing a hunter green v-neck sweater that she'd given him. It brought out the green in his eyes. He pulled her in for a hug and a grateful kiss.

"Thank you so much for coming. You have no idea how much I was looking forward to this day."

"Of course." She smiled and gave him another quick kiss. "I've been looking forward to it a bit, too."

They chatted easily on the way back to Hyannis. Their conversation was light. Kristen filled him in on all the latest gossip, and he told her funny stories about his time at Murphy House. They stopped at Trader Joe's in Hyannis to stock up on snacks that were much less expensive and not as available on the island. They had some time to kill before the ferry left, so they had a quick bite to eat at Tiki Port, Kristen's favorite Chinese restaurant.

Once they were on the boat, after chatting for a bit, Tyler started to yawn and Kristen suggested he take a nap while she read on her Kindle for a bit. This time, she was able to read instead of wondering about Tyler. She had a good feeling about him. He seemed like the Tyler she first met. And she was optimistic that the month-long stay gave him what he needed to stay sober. He'd been in touch with Scotty, and they were going to a meeting tonight. He wanted her to meet Scotty, finally, which she thought was a good step.

Tyler woke as the boat pulled into the pier. Once it was fully docked, they drove home. She walked him home and showed him the refrigerator which she and Andrew had fully stocked with healthy food—lots of veggies, fruit and bottled water. And ice cream.

"You got my favorite flavor? Mint chocolate chip. You and Andrew, I owe you both so much."

Kristen wrapped her arms around him and hugged him close. "You don't owe me a thing. I just want to do what I can to help you stay healthy and strong. You're important to me."

He touched his lips gently to hers. "Do you have any idea how important you are to me? I was falling in love with you before this all happened and during my time away I realized that I am there. I'm totally in love with you, and I know I don't deserve your love, but I wanted you to know that."

"Don't be ridiculous. Everyone deserves love. And I've more than fallen, too. I love you, Tyler, and I'm so glad you're home."

It was almost four in the afternoon, and Kristen figured Tyler probably wanted to settle back in and get unpacked.

"Do you want to come by for dinner in a while? I could make one of those kitchen sink pasta dishes that you like?"

"I have a better idea. I think I saw some fresh

haddock in the refrigerator. How about letting me cook for you? I can make a decent baked haddock and I have a fridge full of veggies to go with it."

Kristen laughed. "Okay, if you're sure you're up for it?

"Why don't you come by around five thirty? Scotty said he'd be by at seven to go to a meeting with me and I want to introduce you two."

"Perfect. I'll see you then."

AT FIVE THIRTY SHARP, KRISTEN KNOCKED ON TYLER'S door. He hollered for her to come in, and she stepped inside and took a deep breath. Something smelled wonderful, lots of butter and lemon. Her stomach growled in anticipation. Tyler was in the kitchen with the oven door open, checking the haddock.

"It should be ready in a few minutes. What is that?"

Kristen held out a bag of chocolate chip cookies. She had them in the freezer and took them out to thaw when she got home earlier.

"Dessert. Leftover cookies."

"Excellent. Help yourself to whatever you want to drink. I'd offer you wine, but as you can imagine there's none of that in the house."

"I don't need wine. Water is perfectly fine." Kristen set the cookies on the counter and grabbed a bottle of water. "Can I do anything to help?"

"Sure. Do you want to find some salad dressing in the fridge? The salads are all set." She found a bottle of Italian dressing and set it by the two salads.

"Those are impressive." The salads weren't your typical garden salads. They were full of all kinds of interesting things—artichoke hearts, chick peas, sliced avocado, bits of blue cheese and crumbled bacon.

"I like a good salad. And you guys put all this cool stuff in the fridge so we have to take advantage."

A few minutes later, Tyler pulled a sheet pan of roasted potatoes and baked haddock out of the oven.

"Are those Ritz crackers?" She'd once told him that was the secret to her mother's seafood stuffing.

"Is there any other way? Butter, lemon and crushed Ritz crackers. I've made it a bunch of times now. It's hard to screw up and is delicious."

They ate at Tyler's island and it was almost like he'd never relapsed. She helped him clean up when they were done and as they were finishing up, there was a knock on the door and she realized it was probably Scotty, Tyler's sponsor. As much as she wanted to meet him, it was also a reminder that Tyler had relapsed and even though he seemed perfectly fine now, it was going to take work to stay there.

Scotty walked in holding a gallon of mint chocolate chip ice cream and handed it to Tyler. "Welcome home."

Tyler pulled him in for a quick hug. "Thank you."

He took the ice cream and put it next to the other gallon in the freezer.

"Scotty, this is Kristen. Kristen, Scotty. You guys are two of the most important people in my life. I thought it was about time you met."

"It's good to meet you. Tyler talks about you a lot." Scotty reached out his hand and Kristen shook it. His hand was strong and calloused. She wasn't sure what he did for work, but guessed it was something physical.

"I've heard a lot about you, too."

"You're Chase's sister, right?"

Kristen nodded.

"I do some work with him from time to time. I'm an electrician." He reached in his wallet and pulled out a business card and handed it to her. "My cell phone is on there, just in case you ever need to reach me for anything." Tyler nodded as she took the card.

"Hopefully you'll never need to call Scotty or my brother about me again, but just in case."

"And on that note, we should head off to that meeting. Nice to meet you, Kristen."

"I'll call you later." Tyler gave her a quick kiss, and she walked out with them and headed home.

CHAPTER 26

A week before Chase and Beth were supposed to close with their buyers, Lauren called with some frustrating news. Chase had stopped into the office for lunch and thought Lauren was calling with good news and put her on speakerphone.

"I've been dreading this call all day. I was hoping that a miracle would happen and they'd get it figured out, but your buyers just let me know that despite their pleading, the bank has declined to finance the mortgage for the house. They're out."

"What about the other couple, that had the cash offer? Can we see if they might still be interested?" Beth asked.

"Or should we do another open house? I hate to lose the twenty thousand," Chase said.

"We could do that, but there're no guarantees we'll get another offer that fast, let alone a cash offer. Realistically, you're probably looking at another month or two at least unless that couple is still interested and you are willing to accept their offer."

Chase glanced at Beth and she nodded. She'd wanted to take the cash offer from the beginning.

"Okay, please see if that couple is still interested," Chase said.

"Will do. Stay tuned.."

"Well, that stinks. I thought we'd be closing next week." Chase stood and crumpled his bag of chips and tossed it in the trash. "I'm going to head back out to the job site. I'll keep you posted if Lauren calls."

LATER THAT AFTERNOON, CHASE CALLED WITH AN update.

"The cash buyers are out—they are closing on a different property next week. That could have been us."

Beth resisted the urge to say, "I told you so."

"So, Lauren will do another open house then? It's a great property, I'm sure we'll have more interest. Nothing we can do about it, except cross our fingers and hope Lauren can get it done again."

"Right. She said she'll do one next Saturday so we'll wait and see."

"The Nantucket Affair event is that night. Would be great to have something to celebrate.

SATURDAY AFTERNOON, AFTER THE OPEN HOUSE, WHILE Beth was being lazy on the living room sofa, clicking the remote and catching up on episodes of the reality show Bachelor in Paradise, Chase's cell phone rang. He'd left it on the coffee table while he was in the shower. The water stopped as the phone rang and Beth saw from the caller ID that it was Lauren. She hollered for Chase to hurry. He ran out of the bathroom, wrapped in a towel and answered the phone on speaker.

"Hi Lauren, please tell us you have good news?"

"Well, I'm not calling with an offer, but I am calling to let you know that not one, not two, but three different clients said they are going to be making an offer. They all know there's multiple interest, so they said they'd get back to me later today with specifics."

"That's great news," Beth said.

"It is. And I think you might be pleasantly surprised by one of them, but I don't want to get your hopes up so I'm not saying anything more until I have an official offer. Are you both going to be at A Nantucket Affair tonight?"

"We are," Chase answered for both of them.

"Good. I'll have my cell of course and if the offers come in the way we want them, maybe we'll be drinking champagne!"

CHAPTER 27

"Curt really outdid himself this year. Everything looks stunning. And we got very lucky with the weather. It couldn't be more perfect tonight." Lisa took a sip of her chardonnay and gazed around the beach, where several huge white and gray tents were set up and what looked like hundreds of tables, all covered in snowy linens, flowers and vintage lanterns with candles inside. The dress was 'creative black tie' so there was a sea of gorgeous dresses on the women and distinguished suits on the men. Tuxedo clad waiters strolled by with silver platters of mouth-watering hors d'oeuvres.

"He really did," Sue agreed as she selected a mini-crab cake from one of the passing platters.

"Did I hear my name?" Curt laughed as he finished talking with someone and turned toward Lisa, Sue and Paige. Rhett and Peter were off getting drinks and all of Lisa's kids and their partners were floating around the event somewhere.

"I was just saying you did a great job, Curt. This is lovely."

He beamed, and Lisa knew the compliment was appreciated. "Thank you. We had an excellent team, and it was a lot of fun to make it happen. Oh, will you ladies excuse me? I see someone I need to go talk to."

Lisa noticed that Curt gave Sue a quick kiss before he left them, and she'd also noticed lately that the vibe between them seemed different. They both looked happier.

"Things seem good with you and Curt?"

"They are much better. Going into the office helped, and brought us closer together. We're both making more of an effort and have had a few date nights recently. I forgot how much fun dating used to be." She smiled and Lisa was happy for her.

"How's Rhett doing with his mask? Is it getting any better? Peter mentioned he called a few weeks ago and was frustrated," Paige asked.

"Much better. He just had to get used to it. He still pulls it off sometimes in his sleep, but he's better with it than he used to be and he admitted that he feels better now. More rested, which is the most important thing."

"Oh, there's Kristen and Tyler with Kate and Jack. The girls look gorgeous, they're both so slim," Sue said.

Lisa laughed. "Remember, they are much younger. They do look pretty. And Tyler is doing well, according to Kristen. He goes to more meetings now and that helps to keep him on track."

"Good. They seem so well suited, both being artists and all. I hope it works out for them," Paige said.

Lisa looked over at Kristen and Tyler. He had his hand lightly on the back of her dress and she was looking up at him with so much love in her eyes. They seem to have gotten more serious since his relapse, and Lisa hoped that it would work out for them.

"Who is that guy that Brandi is with? I thought she was dating John? This guy looks more her age," Lisa asked as Brandi and her date came towards them.

"Funny story there, you'll see in a minute." Sue smiled and greeted Brandi as she walked over to say hello. She introduced everyone.

"Lisa and Paige, this is Brandi. She works in the office with us and Jordan is John's son."

"Nice to meet you," Brandi said.

Lisa couldn't help herself. She had to ask, "How did you two meet?"

"Through the agency, sort of. I was helping John with a new policy and dropped off some papers at his house for him to sign, and Jordan was there. We've been spending time together ever since." She beamed up at Jordan, and he smiled shyly and looked around the room.

"Well, we should go find Jordan's friends. We were supposed to meet them by the bar."

"Have fun," Sue said.

"So, you two are friends now?" Paige asked.

"Sure. Work friends. She's a good kid. And I definitely approve of Jordan over John."

"Are Chase and Abby coming tonight, too?" Sue asked as she snagged a scallop and bacon appetizer as another server with a platter full of food walked by.

"They should both be here somewhere. Abby might be running a little late. She was having some sitter issues. Her usual sitter wasn't available."

Sue laughed. "You mean you?"

"Yep. They don't really go out often enough. I'm always happy to watch Natalie if I'm available."

BETH AND CHASE WERE STANDING AROUND A COCKTAIL table with Angela and Philippe. Philippe looked very theatrical with his dark hair and black tie with deep purple accents. Angela was the opposite, understated and elegant in a long, cream strapless cocktail dress with a double strand of milky pearls.

Beth looked around for Lauren, but didn't see her anywhere yet. Beth knew she was likely on her way, though, if she wasn't already here. She finally spotted Lauren about twenty minutes later. She was hard to miss.

Lauren was in the highest heels Beth had ever seen. Walking looked dangerous. Her dress was beautiful and daring. All white, it had a boat neck top in the front and an almost backless back. With her very blonde hair, Lauren stood out. She waved when she saw them, but didn't come their way for almost an hour. And when she did, she looked excited.

"Chase, Beth, can I talk to you two for a minute?"

They told the others they'd be right back and followed Lauren to an empty high-top table.

"Okay, as I said might happen, we have multiple offers. All good offers. The first two are within five thousand of each other, both right at asking price. So, that's great. They both need financing."

Chase and Beth glanced at each other. Neither was keen for a repeat of what had just happened. Though they knew it was unlikely to happen again quite like that.

"And then we have one cash offer, from the same couple that offered before."

"I thought they bought something else?" Beth said.

"They did. But it was a contingency sale. Their seller had another property fall through, so they backed out."

"Did they offer same as before?" Chase looked somewhat dubious now that they had three offers on the table.

"No. They knew there were three bidders and they were disappointed that they missed out before. They offered the price you counter offered, so twenty thousand higher than before. They really want the house."

Chase grinned. "Well, I have no hesitations, then. Beth, what do you think?"

"I'm thinking it's time for some champagne. Congrats to all of us!"

KRISTEN AND TYLER WERE AT A COCKTAIL TABLE WITH Kate and Jack. Kristen stood close to Tyler, and he wrapped his arm around her shoulders and pulled her close. It was their first night out on the town since Tyler came home from rehab. She'd worried a little that so many people, mostly all drinking, might be stressful for him, but he assured her that he'd be fine. And to look at him now he looked positively zen, and was content people-watching and enjoying the weather and good food.

"I took a spin by the silent auction table about ten minutes ago. Your painting has a lot of bids. I'm not surprised. That's one of my favorites." Kristen had donated one of her paintings for the silent auction. It was a seascape inspired by the coffee-table book of photographs that Tyler had given her.

All proceeds went to the event charity, so it was for a good cause. Plus, as Andrew pointed out, it was also excellent advertising for her show at his gallery tomorrow. He predicted that lots of people that saw the painting, and especially those that bid and lost, might stop by the gallery to see what else was available. The winners of the silent auction items were going to be announced after the fireworks, which would begin as soon as it got dark.

Kristen smiled as she looked at her twin sister. Kate and Jack looked like they had been together forever. For the first time, Kristen couldn't find one wrong thing with one of Kate's boyfriends. Everyone liked Jack, and they'd known him forever. Although she'd felt awful for her sister at the time, Kristen was glad that Kate lost that job at the Boston fashion magazine. She liked having Kate back on the island and now that she and Jack were together, Kristen didn't think she had to worry about Kate moving back to Boston anytime soon.

The fireworks were spectacular. There were soft breezes blowing over the beach and the skies were clear. When they finished, everyone cheered and clapped, and then Jack surprised all of them by pulling a small box out of his pocket and getting down on one knee. Kate looked completely shocked. It was clear she had no idea this might happen tonight.

It was still just the four of them standing there, and Jack looked around the table at all of them before continuing.

"Kate, in front of the people we both love and on the most beautiful night, I thought it was appropriate to tell you how I really feel. I love you, Kate Hodges, more than I thought I could love anyone. You're my best friend and the woman I want to grow old with. Will you marry me, Kate?"

He opened the box and the diamond inside was so pretty. Kristen guessed that maybe it had been his grandmother's. The setting was vintage filigree, and the stone was a lovely oval shape. By the look in Kate's eyes, she liked it too.

"Jack, I did not see this coming. Yes, of course I'll marry you!"

Jack slid the ring on her finger and after a happy kiss, Kate led the way to go find the others. Kristen and Tyler followed along, and they found the whole family gathered near the silent auction tables.

Kate walked over to her mother and the rest of the family and just lifted up her hand and waved it slowly. Screaming and congratulations followed.

Lisa pulled her in for a hug. "What a perfect night for a proposal. I am so happy for you, honey." She reached for Jack and pulled him in, too. "And just as happy for you. Welcome to the family."

Once the excitement died down a little, they brought their attention to the silent auction winner announcements. Kristen was curious to see who ended up winning her painting. When they announced the name, she was shocked at first and then burst into laughter. She looked at Tyler and shook her head.

"I can't believe you bought that painting. You must have overpaid for it."

"It's for a good cause. And once I saw it, there was no question that I had to have it."

"I would happily give you any of my paintings." She didn't even want to think of how much he might have paid.

"I wanted that one. It's special. I loved that image from the book I gave you. I see it as a sign of new beginnings and of our future together. It's going in my living room, or maybe the bedroom. What do you think?"

"I think you're crazy. But, I love you for it. It has been an amazing night for all of us."

CHAPTER 28

The day after A Nantucket Affair, Sue and Curt both slept in, but by a quarter to eleven, Curt put Betty's top down and they drove to Dover Falls to visit with her mother and take her for her promised spin.

The weather was perfect for it. Sunny and warm, with not a cloud in the sky and no wind. Sue put her hair in a ponytail and tied a colorful scarf on like a headband, to keep her hair in place as they drove along. She glanced over at Curt. He looked more handsome than ever to her lately. She'd taken her mother's advice to heart and tried to make more of an effort to do more with Curt and to communicate better. She told him all the time how handsome he looked and realized he'd been starved for that kind of attention.

He'd admitted one night, when they were having a romantic dinner downtown at Keeper's restaurant, that he had liked the attention that Brandi gave him. He knew it wasn't romantic and he didn't want that, but he did like the positive reinforcement from all the women in his life when he dropped the weight and got in shape.

"Brandi can't hold a candle to you, Sue. You're still the only one that I look for when I walk in a room. It's always just been you." Though Sue knew that deep down, it was still nice to hear it again. And she understood how he was looking for that same kind of reinforcement. It was so true that when they both worked at making things better, they ended up happier than either had expected.

Curt pulled up to the front door and left the car running while they went in to get Sue's mother. She must have been watching from an inside window though because as they walked toward the front door, it opened and Sue's mother walked toward them.

"It's about time you brought that fancy car here. How are you both today?" Sue noticed her mother look at the two of them with interest. Curt had his arm around Sue and she smiled back at him as he greeted her mother.

"It's a perfect day for a drive with my two favorite and very beautiful ladies. Would you like to meet Betty and go for a spin?"

Sue's mother laughed. "Betty. I love it." She looked at both of them, and seemed quite pleased with herself. "Yes, there's nothing I'd like more."

THANK YOU SO MUCH FOR READING! I REALLY HOPE YOU enjoyed the story. Next up is a standalone book, also set on Nantucket, about three sisters that inherit a restaurant. One of them, Mandy Lawson, was mentioned in A Nantucket Affair.